Hawaiian Princesses

<u>Books and Stories by Ron Mueller</u>

<u>The Taelo Series</u>

Taelo: The Early Years
Taelo: The Golden Feather
Taelo: Journey of Discovery
Taelo: Dangerous Passage
Taelo: Condor Clan Slingers
Taelo: Circumvention
Taelo: The Journey of Sages
Taelo: Collection
Taelo: Future Leaders Journey

<u>A Taelo Story:</u>

White Swan and Quiet Pheasant
The Child's Name
Floating Cloud
Quiet Rabbit
Busy Bee
Little Otter & Talking Wren
Broken Spear
Burley Bear & Meadow Flower
A Taelo Story Collection

<u>Science Fiction</u>

The Savitar Series:
    Journey's End
    Savitar
    Confluence
    Savitar Collection

Bram Nielson Series
    The Fold
    The Message
    Fold Wormhole
    Negative Fold
    Ripples in Time
    Bram Nielson Collection

<u>Single Science Fiction Books:</u>

    Current Past and Future
    The Event
    The Door
    Viajante 7

Ron Mueller

<u>Fiction Series</u>

The Alex Evercrest Series
    The River Front
    The Girl on The Grill
    Missing
    Maggot
    Racist
    Votive Candles
    Windy City
    Country Road
    Pool of Blood
    Sins of the Daughter
    Body Parts
    The Skull Collector
    The Vanishing
    The Shadow Fighter
    Moonshine
    Grief's Trajectory
    The Magic Touch
    Alex Evercrest Heroine
    Alex Evercrest Collection Two
    Northern Lights

A Brian Oneil Novell
    Hawaiian Phoenix
    Moon Curser
    Death Broker
    Hawaiian Princesses

The Problem Solver Series
    Solutions
    Drug Lords
    Border Crosser
    Problem Solver Collection

Imagination by Courtney Huynh and Chloe Parker

Hawaiian Princesses
By: *Ron Mueller*

Around the World Publishing LLC
4914 Cooper Road Suite 144
Cincinnati, Ohio 45242-9998

This story is a work of fiction. Names, characters, places, and incidents either are products of the author's imagination or are used fictitiously. Any resemblance to actual events or locales or persons, living or dead, is entirely coincidental.

Hawaiian Princesses, Copyright © 2024

ISBN 13: 978-1-68223-947-6
ISBN 10: 1-68223-947-0

Distributed by Ingram
Alex Evercrest Model By: Pi03@ShutterStock
Yacht By: Paul Vinten @ShutterStock
Cover by: Ron Mueller

Ron Mueller

Hawaiian Princesses

<u>Table of Content</u>

Ron Mueller

<u>Chapter 1: The Kala</u>

They were all walking leisurely down the pier to where Marvin was smiling as he welcomed them to the virgin tour of the "Kala." There were sixteen of them that were going out to celebrate the first excursion of the refurbished yacht that Brian and Kekoa had been gifted by Remi after he had been captured trying to escape in it. The yacht at that time was named "Escape" something that Remi had not been able to do. Brian and Kekoa had renamed it Kala, which meant princess in Hawaiian. It had taken almost a year for it to be repaired, refurbished and then sailed to Maui. Marvin had applied to be its captain. He spent the year becoming a registered sea captain. He and his experienced deck hand had gone to Houston and then brought it back to Maui.

Brian and Kekoa had spent a great deal of time negotiating a place to dock the one-hundred-foot yacht. They had reached agreement to have the yacht anchor in the middle of Maalaea Harbor and be allowed to have it pick up people at one of the piers used by a snorkeling tour business. This arrangement allowed them to keep the yacht in Maui.

They had spent a year preparing for the recommissioning party that they were now going out on. Kekoa had arranged for his aunt to cater the party. He and Brian would provide the mood music on guitar and piano. The baby grand was attached to the deck so that it would not end up causing an accident. There were sixteen people in the party itself, three caterers, Marvin and his deck hand, which meant that twenty-two people were on the trip going around the entire island. The number seemed large but once they all got on board and situated they seemed to disappear.

The early morning sun had not yet cleared Mt. Haleakalā when the Kala left the harbor. This was Marvin's first official trip with passengers on the *Kala*. He had brought the yacht *"Escape"* from Houston and then the final internal refurbishment of the yacht took place, and it was transformed into the *Kala*. He and his deck hand had become close friends as together they monitored the refurbishing.

Marvin was keen on having a smooth trip and making sure that everyone enjoyed the celebration. He had been surprised by Brian's and Kekoa's generosity in both time and money. He had been able to hire one of the most experienced Hawaiian deck hands who was as eager as he to make sure everyone was able to relax and enjoy the cruise.

Had he been able to listen to the conversations going on he would have been surprised by how varied and in some cases personal the conversations were.

Hawaiian Princesses

Alex teased Annie about her husband trying to outdo her with the size of his yacht. She had just bought the Golden Goose which was sixty-five feet in length and she was planning to have a party on it as a celebration. She pointed to the baby grand piano and commented that it was going to be hard for her to put anything like that on her yacht. Additionally, she did not have an island like Maui to sail around and was only planning to take her guests out onto Lake Michigan to fish.

A few moments later she got into a serious conversation with Linda and Lorie about their desire to become detectives. This led her to agree to spend some time with the two of them on the following day.

Aurea was the youngest person on the yacht and wandered around to see what the bedrooms and the internal part of the yacht was like. She was a little bored, but she found the snacks were delicious and she filled her plate and went up to the bridge where Marvin was located and sat down in the chair next to him and asked questions about what she saw along the shoreline.

It wasn't long before Sister Ella joined the two on the bridge and engaged Aurea in conversation. She was curious about Aurea being adopted by Alex and wondered how that had come about. She was surprised at the Aurea's confidence and astute description of how it had all come about. She commented that a helping hand from above had taken her to the right home.

Aurea smiled and replied that was most likely true, but it was the heart of a woman she now called mother that had made it all possible.

Sister Ella nodded and said that she had also witnessed how her mother, Alex, had made a difference on the Island as well.

Marvin had been quite during the exchange, and he looked at Aurea with new appreciation for how mature such a young person could be.

Leilani, David, and Malia were enjoying a cool one and discussing the Pool of Blood case that Alex had helped them solve. It had resulted in all three of them being promoted, receiving a bonus, and moving to Honolulu. They were still operating as a team but now had jurisdiction over all the islands. They agreed that it had been a life-changing experience.

Matt was sitting with Kekoa and Brian and sharing the fact that he and Alex were planning to move to her parent's home in Evanston. He shared that Alex had purchased the marina where the Golden Goose was anchored and that he planned to become the skipper of the yacht. When asked what Alex would be doing, Matt smiled and said that he was going to let Alex share that information.

Kaia and Anokoni had been listening to several of the on-going conversations. They looked at each other, Kaia smiled and said that she was glad that they were in business of taking care of young kids at their Day Care and didn't have to deal with the complexities of the lives of the adults around them.

Lunch time found the yacht on track to make it around the island by late into the afternoon. Alex chose that time to share the fact that she was planning to leave her position as a lead detective in Cincinnati and move to Evanston. She shared that she had bought the marina where her father kept his boat. She was planning to hold a celebration and a fishing trip out on Lake Michigan, and they were all invited. She then added that she was going into private practice as an investigator and was working on cementing some deals with the state of Illinois. She laughed and added that unlike, Brian and Kekoa she did not have the multi-billions that they had amassed, and she would have to do real work.

Annie laughed and added that she agreed that Brian and Kekoa seemed to have too much time to sit by the pool doing their hard seemingly non-existent work.

A short time later Alex was cornered by Lorie and Linda. They both asked if they could join her in her private practice.

Alex smiled and replied that if they were serious they should sit down in the next few days and discuss how that might work.

Brian had overheard the conversation and asked if he could join in so he could relax about where his two princesses were going.

The three of them looked at each other, Lorie shrugged and said that it would be a good idea.

Alex suggested they meet at her place for the discussion and afterwards she would grill some fish and vegetables for lunch. And after lunch they could go for a swim from her private beach.

Marvin announced over the speaker that he was slowing down for the last part of the cruise so everyone that wanted to could try their hand at fishing.

Alex took up a pole strapped into the fishing chair and cast it out behind the yacht. She was chatting with Matt when suddenly she got a hit. If she hadn't been wearing her seat belt she would have ended up in the water.

Marvin saw the action and slowed down enough so that Alex and the fish which he thought was a yellow fin tuna known in Hawaiian as Ahi could fight it out. It took about thirty minutes for the fish to be alongside. It was a large one.

He asked if Alex wanted it mounted and smiled when she said that she had plans to put part of it on her grill the following day. He liked the fact that the fish would end up being eaten and not as a trophy on the wall. He called ahead to have the local fish house be at the pier to handle it.

There were two Wahoo known locally as Ono caught before they made the harbor. Matt caught one of them and Alex decided that it would be the one that got grilled for lunch. She arranged for the Ahi to be cut up and a portion given to each of the guests on the boat.

Hawaiian Princesses

When they were dropped off at the pier, Alex posed with the Ahi she had caught and had a picture taken. The Ahi was as long as Alex was tall. It looked like she had caught a giant-sized fish.

Annie asked if it was OK for her to come over with Brian and while the discussion about what Linda and Lorie had in mind she would prepare the lunch with Matt.

On the drive home Matt commented that their lives were taking on a very different path than the last time they had vacationed on Maui.

Aurea asked if she was part of the difference.

Alex laughed and looked at her and said that there was no doubt that she was the most important difference. She had changed her, and Matt's lives in a dramatic and wonderful direction. And this Maui vacation with her was a very enjoyable one and one that she hoped would be memorable to her.

Aurea nodded and commented that she was happy that she had been left on the porch of very successful and rich parents. Parents that could afford a magnificent home on the Maui waterfront. Have a black Jaguar in Evanston and a red one on Maui. Be able to take her out to great restaurants and surfing from their home.

She then added that now she would have to get use to fishing off of a boat called the *"Golden Goose"*, but she preferred her grandfather's smaller boat which she had named the *"Minnow"*. She added that she was going to apply to work in the bait house.

Alex smiled and said that the new owner would consider her application for a job as long as homework got done and grades were kept up.

Aurea stood up and gave both of them a hug and said that she loved them.

Alex said that she was a treasure that needed to get her seatbelt back on.

They got to the house and they all carried in the food that they had been given when they got off the yacht.

Alex suggested that they put everything on the kitchen table, get their swimsuits on and go for a quick swim before they got dinner prepared.

That night she and Matt lay in bed talking. She asked if he was OK with all the changes that were going to be happening.

Matt said that he was more than OK, but he was worried that she would be working in an area of the country where she had faced some of her more threatening scenarios. He made the point that Evanston was nothing more than a northern part of Chicago. He added that he was going to have a much less stressful job, and she seemed to be stepping into a much more dangerous situation.

Alex gave a small laugh and commented that she had faced danger across the whole of the US of A, into Mexico, Canada, and Brazil while she had lived in the sleepy little city of Cincinnati. She had run ins with the Chicago Mafia three times during that same period. She shook her head and said that knowing that the Chief, Bob, and Trevor were all retiring meant that the department would take on a totally different culture. She was going to see if Trey and Johnnie would want to join her organization and move with her to Evanston.

Matt said that he understood her desire to get back to her hometown where they could raise Aurea in a place where she would have similar experiences to that which she had experienced with her father.

Alex nodded and said that her early years with her father and mother had molded her and given her confidence throughout her career. She wanted Aurea to experience the same thing with the two of them.

Matt smiled and said that he was looking forward to having those experiences with Aurea and he agreed with Aurea that they were rich.

Chapter 2: The Discussion

Alex was preparing some pancake mix when she looked out the window and saw that Aurea was not in bed as she had been thinking but was fishing near the end of the opening that led away from the house out to the ocean. She watched as Aurea caught what turned out to be a nice sized sea bass. It seemed clear to her that Aurea enjoyed fishing as much as she did.

Aurea came into the house with a big smile as she put the fish into the sink. She said that she was going to clean and prepare it to be grilled for lunch.

Alex went over and complimented her on the great catch and gave her a hug. She complemented her on getting up early to do some fishing. She suggested that after she got her fish cleaned and sautéed she get ready for a pancake, egg, and sausage breakfast.

Aurea smiled and added that the pancakes would get smothered in lots of syrup.

Matt came down to the kitchen and helped himself to a cup of coffee and asked if there was a nice hot pancake or two for him. He walked around and gave everyone a hug, saw the fish in the sink and asked who had been up early enough to go fishing.

Aurea said that she had caught the bass and was planning to have it, some grilled corn, and other grilled vegetables for lunch.

"Well, you can work with the grill master who will get everything ready for the grill and later you can be sure to time how long to grill everything," Matt replied as he put butter and syrup on his pancake. He broke the over easy egg and watched the yolk slowly spread out over the syrup-soaked pancake. This was one of his favorite breakfasts. He got a combination of pancake and egg to his mouth with his fork, said it was a great way to wake up as he took a sip of his coffee.

Only a few miles away, Linda and Lorie were sitting in their apartment discussing their desire to work with Alex. Both of them considered her their aunt and called her that. They had fond memories of growing up in Cincinnati and often being visited by Alex and Matt. They agreed that Matt was their favorite "uncle" to play with.

They were in the process of setting up a private detective office and were trying to get clients. One of their friends had introduced them to an acquaintance who said that she had been raped and that she had filed a complaint that had never been followed up on by the police.

Friends in Cincinnati had also sent them a few potential clients.

They had done their homework and knew that they were just two more people in a sea full of many young men and a few other women trying to get into the same field. They had talked about applying to some up and running private investigative firms but knew that they once again would be vying against many people trying to do the same thing and in that endeavor they were not sure if they would fit the mold that the investigative firm might want.

They were now discussing how they could get their aunt to hire them or be partners with them and somehow help them get their feet on the ground. They agreed that getting an opportunity with her would be the greatest thing that could happen.

Just down the hill from their apartment building, Brian and Annie were having a conversation that very closely mirrored Linda's and Lorie's but from the perspective of concerned parents. Both of them wanted their daughters to be successful even though they wished that the two were choosing to go into painting or some profession other than private investigators.

Brian commented that the two did not actually need to work but had refused to accept living off the fortune that he and Kekoa had amassed.

Annie responded that she understood and respected their two daughters desire to be on their own. She said that made her proud and she was sure the two would be successful once they got their feet on solid ground. She hoped that Alex would provide some guidance and perhaps be a bridge to that solid ground.

Back in her oceanside house, Alex closed her eyes and relaxed in the shade on the reclining chair. She loved the back yard and the variety of plants that provided the shade. Her favorite were the small coconut trees with small coconuts that were just getting ripe. She loved the sweet juice of when she chewed on them.

Her mind was on what Linda and Lorie were likely to ask. She knew they were very good artists but were also into the intrigue that their father, Brian was into, in his quest for wayward billionaires. She wished the two had followed Annie into being artists but knew that it would be as hard for them to get started there as it would be to get started as independent investigators. But she knew that art was dramatically less dangerous then being an investigative detective.

She had thought about how she could help the two. It depended on the work relationship the two wanted to set up. She had been on the gun range with them and knew they were both excellent shots and both owned the latest top end revolvers.

They had both graduated close to the top of their classes. Linda had a BS in Finance and Lorie had a BS in Mechanical Engineering and both had minored in art. She knew from talking with Johnnie that the two were very good at surfing the internet in search for information. There was no doubt in her mind that the two were very talented.

She was not surprised when Annie came around the side of the house carrying a dish. She was followed by Linda, Lorie and Brian all carrying a dish of some sort. She got up and led the way into the house and had them put the food on the kitchen table.

Aurea lifted the lid of each dish and commented that they would all go well with the fish and vegetables that they would grill for lunch.

Matt welcomed everyone and said that he was leading the way out for a swim and then when he got back he would get the grill fired up and get lunch set up in the backyard.

Alex suggested that Linda, Lorie, and Brian pour themselves a glass of lemonade or iced tea and follow her to the lounge chairs in the back yard. Once they were all seated she asked Linda and Lorie to share what they had in mind.

Linda shared that she and Lorie had talked about having offices in Oahu, and Cincinnati where they hoped to get coaching from her. They were both open to some sort of business relationship but would be honored if they could be junior partners in her new investigative practice that she was starting in Evanston.

Alex said that she had thought about how the three of them might work together. She suggested that they become junior partners in a firm that might be called Evercrest and O'Neil. They would begin by becoming licensed private investigators in the states of Hawaii, Ohio, and Illinois.

This would require them to get an associate degree in police science, criminal law, or justice and two and a half years of experience.

She as the senior partner, a licensed PI in all states, would be the one certifying their qualification. During their qualification period they would be carrying out duties such investigating crimes, investigating identities, business, occupation, character, of a person, investigating the location of lost or stolen property, investigating the cause of fires, losses, accidents, damage or injury, and securing evidence for use in court.

She smiled and asked if they would be able to handle many hours of boredom and chasing leads to dead ends.

Linda and Lorie looked at each other then asked Brian why he had chosen to become a private investigator.

Brian shook his head and said that it was because of the fact that he had wondered who his father was and spent his time finding that out. The fact that his father was a very wealthy person who hand never sought him out made him wonder why. Trying to answer that question led him to the discovery of very wealthy people preying and taking advantage of people who were in special situations that could be profitable to them. He added that he had been lucky three times and had amassed a great deal of money. But he and Kekoa seemed to have a two- or three-year dry period between cases so they had been lucky to have made a great deal of money from the very first case.

Alex gave a small laugh and said that perhaps she should chase a wayward billionaire for the Evercrest and O'Neil Agency's first case so they could all handle the dry period between cases. She said that she had a paying position with the state of Illinois in the office of the Lieutenant Governor as a licensed police investigator. She added that the Hawaii home they were currently at generated enough income to cover the salary that she was going to offer them as junior partners.

She then asked the two if they had any questions.

Lorie asked about the idea of having an office on Oahu and Cincinnati.

Alex nodded and said that having one in Oahu, one in Cincinnati and one in Evanston would be the setup she had in mind. She looked at Brian and added that she did not want to compete with him on Maui.

Brian chuckled and said that he did not want to compete so low on the financial ladder, so he would stay to the upper financial stratosphere.

Linda spoke up and said that an Oahu office would allow her and Lorie to get their associate degree in police science, criminal law, or justice. A Cincinnati office would allow them to keep in contact with their friends there and working with her in Evanston would let them get her direct coaching.

Alex smiled and added that the home in Cincinnati would be lived in by one of their special friends, Nolan, who she had hired to take care of the place and the current art that would remain on the third floor for the immediate future. She added that the house had plenty of room for the two of them to have a place in Cincinnati and they could work from home and did not need to have the expense of an office.

When they were in Evanston they could stay at her home and have desks at her office. She had not yet found an office there but would make sure that she had the expansion space for a successful business with at least two partners.

She asked what their salary expectations were.

Lorie looked at Linda who shook her head and answered that they had researched what detectives and investigators made and hoped to make above the average.

Alex knew the range across the US and offered to pay a flat one-hundred-thousand dollars plus health and dental care.

Both Lorie and Linda smiled and said that they were happy to become junior partners in Evercrest and O'Neil Investigators.

Brian congratulated the two and said that he was throwing in free transportation to Cincinnati and Evanston for at least a year as a career launch gift.

Alex gave the two hugs and said that there would be many details that they would need to work through, but they would take that one step at a time.

Aurea came into the backyard and said that the swim had been great, and that five turtles were eating seaweed at the end of the opening.

Matt led the way to the freshwater shower, and everyone took turns showering.

Annie could tell that Linda and Lorie were very happy and figured that Alex had given them what they were looking for. It was hard for her not to ask but she was going to wait for them to share what had happened. She went into the house and prepared the food so each person could serve themselves and then go out and sit at the picnic table.

Matt fired up the grill and Aurea brought out the fish, sausage and cut vegetables.

Soon everyone was seated, and Matt asked if the talk had gone well.

Linda smiled and said that their aunt had once again saved her and Lorie by opening a door that they had only dreamt about. She then elaborated on the details and the fact that they were going to be paid top dollar to live their dream.

<u>Chapter 3: Oahu</u>

Brian and Annie left the gathering at Alex's house pleased with the outcome of the discussion that Linda and Lorie had with Alex. He commented that the one specific requirement that Alex had insisted on was that Linda and Lorie each needed to paint their favorite scene for each of their office locations as part of the partnership agreement and that in each of the next three years each of them needed to paint at least one additional painting of some scene associated with their work.

Annie laughed and said that sounded like Alex. She was leaving the door open for either of them to choose to go another way. She added that in any future art show that she sponsored, Linda's and Lorie's paintings would be shown. Maybe one of the two would be found and chose painting as the path they enjoyed more than investigating.

She added that the requirement to get certified and licensed as registered detectives kept the two in Hawaii a few years longer. That again was something that she liked. Finally, she said that she liked the fact that in both Oahu and in Cincinnati the two would be able to work from home and did not need to set up offices. It was clear to her that Alex had thought through how she would work with Linda and Lorie. She added that she could not think of a better person for them to work with or for because they would be working with someone of high integrity, a person that would have deep feelings for them and a person who would make sure she developed them.

Brian said that he felt the same way. He had offered them the plane that he leased as a means of making their transition easier. He would have liked to do more because he certainly had the means to do so but he also knew that the two would have turned any more financial aid down. He was pleased that Alex acknowledged the offer and said that she would gladly accept it because it would make the entire enterprise more competitive and certainly would make long distance travel easier. She had later explained that the business entity would need to make the appropriate legal arrangements for the use of the plane so it could be reported on the tax forms.

Hawaiian Princesses

Linda and Lorie left Alex's house in a high. They decided to go out and celebrate. They called several of their friends and chose their favorite place that was only a few blocks from their apartment. They walked there and felt free to enjoy a few glasses of wine and dance with their friends. The evening walk back to their apartment was a slow and easy walk as they took in the mirid of stars that seemed to be sparkles of joy to both of them.

Alex spent the rest of the evening sitting on the second-floor veranda watching the sun slowly flowing toward the horizon. She watched Aurea reading a book and snacking on the popcorn that they had popped before sitting down. Matt was sitting by her side, and they were holding hands.

He commented that things for their transition to a new life were falling into place in a nice way.

Alex nodded and said that indeed it seemed so. She hoped it would continue to keep falling smoothly into place. She needed to find an appropriate office in the Evanston area that had enough space for at least ten people.

Matt asked why she would need a space for ten people.

Alex gave a light laugh and said that she already had four people in the office. She added that for sure she wanted to entice two more people before she opened her office.

Matt asked who the two happened to be.

She said that she was pretty sure he knew who they were.

Aurea looked up from her book and said that she would guess it would be Johnnie and Trey.

Alex nodded and said that indeed she had guessed the right two.

Aurea said that she knew Johnnie would come but she wondered if Trey would be willing to pass up a promotion to do so and how would his salary be covered.

Alex shook her head and replied that Aurea should go back to reading and let her handle the recruiting and handling the finances of the business.

Aurea waved her hand in the air and took a sip of her lemonade and went back to reading.

The next morning, Alex called Linda and asked that as they searched for an apartment on Oahu, that they also search for an office in Evanston in a ten-mile radius of her home address. She gave them the specifications and added that it could be slightly bigger but not smaller. She added that if they found a place, they were invited to go back with her to help set it up.

Linda looked over at Lorie and said that it seemed that it could not get better. They were getting in at the very beginning of a new practice and were being pulled in just as they had hoped they would be.

They not only got online to find their apartment on Oahu but contacted all their friends and acquaintances and let them know that they were looking for clients. They wanted to come into the practice with some of their own cases so they could show Alex that they were worth what she was paying them.

Hawaiian Princesses

The next day they were in Oahu looking at three places that had made their look at list. They spent the day going to each location and after looking at the three places decided that the one closest to the Kahanamoku Lagoon was the one that they would settle on. The apartment was a three bedroom that featured a great room with a small exterior porch and a kitchen that made a person want to cook. It was unfurnished but had all stainless-steel kitchen appliances built in. The apartment was on the top floor and the building had a roof top swimming pool and entertainment area. It was only two blocks away from the Ala Wai Boat Harbor and only a mile away from the Ala Moana Beach. They agreed that it was a place they would enjoy.

They spent another day zeroing out their savings on the furnishings for the apartment. They each picked out their own bedroom furniture and bed. Together they picked out what they wanted in the great room and out on the porch. They hired an interior decorator to review their picks. They knew which paintings they wanted in each room. They would all be ones that their mother had painted.

The evening of the second day they returned to Maui excited about the move.

They then concentrated on finding potential offices in the Evanston area. They zeroed in on three sites.

One was located in an apartment building; had almost a whole floor and each office had a great view of Lake Michigan to the east.

Another was in the same area but did not have the enticing features, but it had a much lower rental cost.

The third one was at ground level, was a large enough building and was within walking distance to the harbor where Alex now owned the Marina and where the *"Golden Goose"* was located. They shared this with Alex and said they were eager to go there and help her with the decision of which one to lease.

Alex was surprised but pleased at how quickly Linda and Lorie were moving. Her vacation was coming to an end. Her parents were arriving and would be staying for two weeks. She would be picking them up and then she would be flying back to the mainland that same day.

She made arrangements with Brian to use the jet he had offered and let him know that Linda and Lorie were returning with her to help establish the office in Evanston.

Brian said he was pleased to make use of the plane that he had on retainer and that in the future she should feel free to make use of it especially to come to Hawaii and spend time with him and Annie. He added that they had plenty of room so if her house was being rented she could stay with them.

Alex thanked him and said that she appreciated that the plane was available to her.

Hawaiian Princesses

Aurea was excited to be staying for the next two weeks with her grandparents. She figured that it was a great way to end her summer. When she went back to the mainland she would be entering a new school and have to make new friends. She knew she was going to be going to the same school that her mother had gone and wondered if some of the older teachers would be the same ones. This would be her third school since she had come to the US. It was hard for her to fathom all the challenges that she had faced and how each had turned out for the best. She wondered what the move north would be like. She had started her journey in Brazil with one set of parents and was now going to live in the northern part of the US with her second set of parents.

Linda and Lorie had spent their time moving out of their Maui apartment and had taken all the stuff they were moving to Oahu to their parent's house. They had piled their belongings in two of the four car stalls. They were exhausted with moving out of their apartments and had made sure that each box was labeled and would not be opened until they were in their new apartments on Oahu. They planned to finalize their move when they returned from the mainland.

Aurea was excited to greet her grandparents. She had purchased leis and was eager to give it to them. She had looked up their meaning and found out that leis was a symbol of love, and it reflected what Aloha meant. She learned that in ancient Hawaii the lei represented wealth, royalty, and rank.

She had also purchased two that she gave to her new mother and father. She was proud that she had purchased them with the money she earned by doing the dishes and helping keep the kitchen clean.

She was standing at the bottom of the escalator when she saw Rose-Anne and Russel Evercrest coming down. She greeted them with a large smile and shouted out Aloha and put the lei over each of their necks. She loved the hugs and kisses she got. She got picked up and carried to the luggage carousel area and put down on the cement bench that went around a set of small palm trees.

Linda and Lorie were there with them because after everything got settled they were flying out with Alex and Matt and going to the house that her grandparents had just left. She smiled at the thought that she was the baton that was being passed to the next set of people that were going to take care of her.

After the luggage arrived and the parting hug and kisses were all done, Alex led the way to security. Once they got through, they were met by Darrel who led them to where their private jet was parked.

Once they got in the air Linda and Lorie shared the pictures of the offices they had found.

They were also excited to have lined up four investigation cases that were not yet under contract but had been referred to them through their friends.

One of the cases that had captured their interest was of an unsolved missing person case. They were eager to discuss this with Alex.

The ten-hour flight was spent sleeping and then a short time before landing Lorie described the three places that they had identified as potential office spaces. They landed at the Chicago Executive Airport and were met there by a taxi driver that Alex had used for many years. He greeted them and put their luggage in the back of the SUV.

Alex thanked him for meeting them and commented on the new SUV he was driving.

He shared that he had recently gone into business on his own and relied on the calls from his many long-time clients. He then verified that Alex wanted to go to her house.

Alex said that she wanted to go drop off all the luggage and then after that she would like him to drive the three of them to look at some office buildings. She gave him the addresses and said that she would call the realtors and make sure they could get in for a viewing then they would head out.

He said that would work for him. He had one pickup immediately after dropping them off and he would then return and wait for them at the front door.

Chapter 4: The Office

After getting her luggage unpacked Alex went to the kitchen, made some coffee, and got a thermal cup full to take with her. She would have preferred taking a nap but figured that it might interfere with getting back into the right sleep cycle.

She contacted each of the realtors and set the time for each location. She planned to spend about an hour at each location to evaluate the location as well as the office area. The one closest to the Marina had a large advantage over the other locations but she wanted to make sure it would be an adequate facility. Since she was prejudiced to that location she put it last in the order of visits.

Matt wished them good hunting and let them know that he was going to go to the Marina and get acquainted with its operation and was planning to sit on the Golden Goose and enjoy the day getting used to it.

The first stop had a whole floor for the office available and had a great view out to the lake. She complimented Linda and Lorie for finding it. In her discussion with the realtor, she found out that the deal was a three-year lease that could be renewed if both sides agreed.

She thanked the realtor and let her know that she would hear from her by the middle of the afternoon.

The second viewing was of a five-story building where the top two floors were available. It met all the requirements but did not have the view that the first showing had. It was offered at half the price of the first office complex and the surrounding area had some of the better restaurants in the area. It had a lower lease cost and was renewable on a yearly basis. This made it slightly more attractive to Alex, but it was still more than she wanted to spend in a business that did not have its first customer.

Alex again let the realtor know that she would make a decision by that afternoon.

It was just before lunch, and she suggested they check out one of the nearby restaurants and afterwards see the last location.

They chose a venue that had an out-door seating area and enjoyed a light lunch. Afterwards they went to the last location.

They arrived at the last location and Alex paid the driver, thanked him for driving, gave him a good tip and said that she would be making arrangements later for him to take the two of them back to the airport in a day or so.

Hawaiian Princesses

The last building was surrounded by trees at the edge of the property and had a large surface parking lot. Alex walked around the edge of the property as they waited for the realtor to show up. She smiled when she saw a walking path that left the property and headed toward the marina. She measured the building to be one hundred paces long and seventy-five paces wide as she walked around the building and decided that the brick needed to be pressure washed and she would have a flower bed that went all the way around it so it would be more attractive. She also thought the windows might need to be upgraded.

The realtor was just getting out of her car when she got back to the front.

After listening to an apology from the realtor for being late, they all went into the building. Its layout left a lot to be desired and Alex was having second thoughts about it. She asked about the rental or lease agreement and learned the current owner would rather sell than lease. Alex asked what the selling price was and was pleased to learn that it was only a seven million three hundred and fifty thousand dollar asking price. She felt that the location made it worth more to her than the asking price. She made the point that it would cost her close to four hundred fifty thousand dollars to modify the interior to fit her needs. She then made a counteroffer of six million one hundred thousand dollars and the sale could be closed that afternoon.

The realtor asked that they wait a moment while she called the owner to find out his reaction to the offer. A few moments later she returned with a smile and said that the owner knew her parents and agreed to sell the place for six million three hundred thousand. He said that he had fished with your father several times, had great memories of those trips, and still remembered the great taste of the fish. He had made the sale contingent on being taken on another fishing trip.

Alex smiled and said that she would make sure to take him and his wife out on a fishing trip that they would remember.

She arranged for a Monday meeting to get the required paperwork initiated and to get the payment arranged.

The realtor said that she was pleased to have met her and was looking forward to getting everything arranged during the following week. She asked if Alex wanted the keys to the building.

Alex thanked her, took the keys, and said she looked forward to getting things closed in the following week.

After the realtor left, Linda asked how Alex was so sure she could cover the asking price so quickly.

Alex smiled and said that she had cleared that with her bank while she was still on Maui. It was the same bank that had financed her Maui and her Cincinnati homes.

She then suggested they walk to the Marina and see if they could figure out what to do for the rest of the afternoon.

Hawaiian Princesses

The walk to the Wilmette Harbor Marina and out on the dock to where the Golden Goose was tied off took less than ten minutes. They found Matt sitting out on the back deck reading and enjoying a glass of lemonade.

Alex gave him a hug and said the three of them were going to order a pizza to be delivered a little later and meanwhile they would join him with a glass of lemonade.

Lorie walked through the Golden Goose and came out and said that it was just like she remembered it. She added that the last time that she had gone out on the Golden Goose she was nine years old, and she remembered having fun fishing and then hearing what she learned were gunshots. She also remembered being grabbed by Alex and being shoved into the kitchen area. She and Linda crawled out to the edge of the kitchen and watched Alex and Trey shooting their weapons at a speed boat that was heading toward land. Then suddenly the Golden Goose lurched forward, and its bow came up out of the water and the water behind it seemed to have a wave that was chasing them.

The next thing she remembered was seeing blood dripping from Alex's left hand and seeing her jump off the boat before it had been tied off at the dock. She saw Alex firing at a figure running up the boat ramp as she ran up the dock toward the parking area. She then saw the police arrive and the paramedics putting a bandage on Alex. She smiled and said that both she and Linda sat in the back of her Jaguar that at that time was green as Trey drove them back to the house.

She stopped and asked if there were any fish in the dock area.

Matt got up and returned with two poles and a multi chambered container that had two different types of worms, a chamber with grubs, one with three live minnows, and another with a handful of crickets.

Lorie thanked him and took the container and the poles to the side opposite of the pier and commenced to prepare her pole. Linda joined her and the two cast their lines out.

It wasn't long before Lorie pulled in a redear sunfish.

Matt took a large square twenty-gallon container where the fish could be put.

Alex watched as both Linda and Lorie alternated catching blue gill and redear. The red spot on the gills of the redear were easy to spot. She was enjoying watching the two fish. She let Matt know that she had agreed to buy a building that was only a ten-minute walk away. It seemed to be in an ideal location, had plenty of room and a large parking lot. She figured that in the future she would turn most of the parking lot into lawn and a rose garden.

He commented that he was pleased that her office would be so close. He let her know that he was taking a group out fishing the following morning.

She asked if he could handle three more people.

He smiled and said that it would be no problem.

Jason, Alex's first police boss now running her mother's pizzeria, delivered the pizza and said that he was pleased to learn that she was moving back into the house she had grown up in. He looked over at Linda and Lorie and asked who the two young women happened to be.

She smiled and said that he should remember them from when they were ten or eleven years old. They had gone out on the Golden Goose the time that a racist had tried to kill her. This was their first time back and they would be joining her in her new business.

Jason commented that time did not hold still but seemed to fly by. He wished them all a good day and headed back to the parking lot.

After Jason left, Alex asked whether Matt would be willing to clean the fish and bring them home. She would fry them along with some vegetables for dinner.

She called Linda and Lorie to get a piece of pizza and let them know that the three of them would return to their new office building and discuss the layout. She let them know that Matt would bring their fish to the house and the fish would be the main course for dinner.

She asked whether they would like to go out fishing on the Golden Goose the following morning.

Linda gave a small laugh and said that she would love to, but she insisted that she go out as a paying customer.

Lorie nodded and said that she too wanted to be a paying customer.

Alex looked at Matt who said that he was planning to give everyone a certificate stating that they were the first paying customers of the new Golden Goose Fishing business. The other six people were from the local area and were responding to the ad he had put in the local paper that offered a fishing trip with lunch for the mere price of one hundred dollars and free bait.

He laughed and added that the money he was getting would just pay for the gas that the Golden Goose would gobble up.

On the walk back to the newly acquired office building, Linda shared the fact that they had four potential cases that her friends had identified. She asked how she and Lorie should handle them.

Alex thanked them for getting started so quickly and said that they would need to get the legal documents that would be used in the practice. They had to get the documents on their company letterhead and then distribute the paperwork to the three offices they would be running. She added that she would contact her mother's law practice and identify the legal documents they would need. Once she did that she would get them printed on the letter head of their new business and distributed. She said that would most likely take another week.

They arrived back at the office building and went in. Alex asked how the offices should be laid out.

Together they discussed the reception area layout. They discussed which direction the main offices should face and where the huddle rooms would be located. Alex suggested that the offices face out to the parking lot area. She shared that she was planning to make most of the parking lot into a garden bordered on each side with a trellis that would have wisteria growing on them and with a flower and herb garden interior. The garden would have several benches located somewhere. She added that she would get a landscape professional to transform the exterior of the building into one that would be pleasing to the eye.

Linda said that sounded great. She was looking forward to the transition.

The layout of the offices was next on the list. Alex said that she wanted to have the corner office farthest from the front door. The next two offices would be for two senior partners and the two offices closest to the front door would be for the two junior partners. All the offices would be the same size with the same basic interior furniture and décor. She would get an interior office decorator to do the layouts. She asked if there were any questions.

Lorie asked who the two senior partners were.

Alex smiled and said that she did not yet have them, but she was after two of her former Cincinnati team members.

Lorie nodded and said that her guess would be Johnnie Smith and Trey McGregor. She had been talking with Nolan and had learned that his father was hesitating to accept becoming Chief of Detectives.

Alex smiled and said that her guess was correct and the information that Nolan had shared with her gave her the impetus to give Trey a call and make him the offer to go into practice with her.

She floated the title of Evercrest, Nolan, Smith, and O'Neil Investigators as the name of their practice.

"A rose is a rose by any other name," Linda said with a smile.

She asked what they would do with the back side of the building.

Alex said that she wanted to have a huddle room across from her office and a huddle room across from Trey's office then a computer room across from Johnnie's office, a spare office across from the next office and a storage room across from the first office. She said that she wanted to have the hall that ran the length of the building be three people wide but have blocking doors that could break the hallway into three sections. The doors would be used for protection if necessary.

The glass windows would be made bullet proof with thick plexiglass mounted on the inside.

Linda asked if she were planning to have attackers that had to be repelled?

Alex shook her head and said that she would be insisting that each of them always act as if someone was out to kill them. She added that wearing personal protective gear would be a requirement and that the bullet proof vest would be worn every day.

Lorie said that she knew that the Kevlar vest that her father had been wearing when he was shot at by an assassin had saved his life and she was all for wearing the outfit. She added that the vest had saved his life more than once, but he had commented that it was not something to be worn in the water.

Alex nodded and said that they should go online and place orders for their Kevlar outfits. She said that her supplier had an online Ap that took the measurements from a selfie and produced perfect fitting outfits.

She then said it was time to go home and sit by the pool, grill some fish and vegies, and enjoy a celebratory glass of wine.

Chapter 5: Senior Partners

Grilling the fish and enjoying sitting at pool side enjoying an iced tea was just the decompression that they needed. The fish, grilled with just some salt and pepper and the grilled vegetables were a great combination. Matt had warmed up a loaf of garlic bread that provided the perfect balance to the rest of the food.

Alex offered Linda and Lorie a choice of wines, but they insisted that they join her with the nonalcoholic version of Lambrusco.

Lorie commented that nonalcoholic would be their choice every time they were together.

Alex called Aurea and her parents during the dinner using a face-to-face Ap and shared their success in finding an office building that was only a ten-minute walk from the harbor.

Aurea asked whether they had taken pictures.

Linda said that she and Lorie had both taken a ton of pictures and sent them out.

Aurea said that the place looked like it had been deserted, the building was out of fashion and the place needed a face lift.

Lorie laughed and said that they were all in agreement and it would be getting a facelift.

The discussion shifted to what Aurea was doing on vacation with her grandparents.

Aurea said that they were learning how to paddle board, and she was able to stand and paddle if she stayed just outside of where the waves seemed to build up before going in to shore.

After talking to Aurea, Alex called Trey and asked him if he would be willing to be a senior partner in her new business.

Trey beamed a huge smile and said that was an offer that he would never turn down.

Lindsey put her head in her hands and started crying. She apologized and said that the request answered one of her prayers. She and Trey had been discussing the fact that on the coming Monday he had been asked to respond to the offer of becoming Chief of Detectives.

Trey spoke up and said that he really had no desire to take that position, but he also did not want to remain as a senior detective in an office where he would be the only remaining person that had been a member in the greatest group of people he had ever worked with. He would love to move to Evanston and be a partner in her new investigative operations.

Lindsey struggled to talk as she said that once again Alex was changing their life's trajectory in the upward direction.

Alex added that she had the funds lined up so that she could offer him a ten percent raise in salary from what he was currently making and in the future they would all share equally in the income of the practice.

Lindsey had been crying the whole time, but she stopped and asked if Alex had a realtor that they could use to find a place to live.

Alex nodded and said that she did and would have her call to get the ball rolling.

They said goodbye and she then called Johnnie.

He answered his phone with, "Mary and I are ready to move to Evanston. Just tell us when."

Alex laughed and said that as soon as they could, would be great.

He replied that they had already made arrangements that Mary's cousin would move into their house which they were planning to keep as a long-term investment. In the short term they were giving her cousin a rent-free home so she could save her money to buy a house of her own.

Alex said that as soon as they found a place in Evanston they could get started.

After the call, Linda commented that she and Lorie were really lucky to have asked to go into practice with her and been accepted.

Alex agreed that if they had not asked she would not have made them an offer. The fact they had been brave enough to ask had made it a very easy decision that she was very confident would yield a significant boost to the effort of setting up their business.

The next day, Linda and Lorie said that they had an appointment to look at an apartment in the first building that they had visited when they were looking for office space. They were planning to rent a three-bedroom apartment that faced the lake on the top floor.

Alex asked if they were meeting with the same realtor and when she found out they were she asked them to let her know that the office in the building was no longer of interest to them.

She contacted the support in her mother's office and asked if she knew of anyone looking for a support role position. She had worked with her mother's support when she had first graduated from law school.

She got three names that might be interested in the role. She hit pay dirt on the third call when she talked with a Marisa Eberly. They agreed to meet for lunch for an interview. Alex chose a restaurant that had a second-floor patio area and had a menu she enjoyed. She arrived early so she could get a table that was in the corner farthest from the entrance area.

Hawaiian Princesses

When Marisa arrived she was pleased to see that she was a person who did not try to look un-aged and who wore a practical black suite outfit. Marisa was half a head taller than she and was on the slender side. She had blue eyes, white hair, and a distinctive narrow nose. Alex put her down as a person who had been very good-looking and who was aging well.

Marisa introduced herself and asked what Alex would like to know about her experience and why she was currently unemployed.

Alex suggested they order lunch first and then they could get into the opportunity she thought might be of interest.

She ordered an eggplant salad, black mussels and for desert she chose mango and passionfruit cream layered crepes and to drink she chose an iced tea.

Marisa chose a shrimp salad, fried mushrooms and chose a chocolate cake for desert and iced tea.

Alex shared the fact that she was opening an office that would house five detectives. She let Marisa know that she also had also purchased Wilmette Harbor Marina that was within walking distance from the building that she had just agreed to purchase. She let her know that she was also an Investigative Marshall in the office of the Illinois Lieutenant Governor.

She then asked Marisa which professor she had worked for at the University.

Marisa smiled and said that before she shared her background she needed to ask if Alex was related to Rose-Anne Evercrest or Professor Evercrest.

Alex smiled, said Rose-Anne was her mother, and her father was a professor at Northwestern University.

Marisa nodded and said that she had supported a professor until he got a position at the University of Illinois in Champaign-Urbana. There were no other positions she wanted to fill so she was out looking on the open market. She shared that she had more than twenty-five years of experience as an office support and before that she had worked in a bakery for a few years. She had never married, had no children, and lived not more than two miles from the restaurant.

Alex knew that the top pay for a senior office support was roughly sixty thousand dollars. She made an offer of seventy-five thousand dollars and watched what Marisa's reaction would be.

Marisa stopped with her fork midway to her mouth and asked if she had heard correctly.

Alex repeated her offer and said that there would be times when she should expect some long hours and hours other than eight to five.

Marisa smiled and said that the offer was very generous, and she was ready to start that very day.

Alex said that after finishing their desert the two of them would go to the building she had just agreed to buy, and she would share the changes she was planning to make to the grounds and to the interior.

She called Linda and Lorie, let them know that she had just hired a support for the office and asked them to meet at the office after they were done with their lunch.

Linda and Lorie looked at each other and said that they needed to get back to Hawaii and get certified as investigators so they could keep up with Alex.

When they walked out to the parking lot and over to a black Jaguar, Marisa walked around it and commented what a beauty the car was.

Alex smiled and said that it was a car that her father had given her when she graduated from high school. It had been old then and now it was an antique that she loved.

When they arrived at the office, Marisa took in the one-story red brick building that was wrapped in windows and had an extra-large parking lot. She thought the building needed a face lift but did not say anything.

Alex led the way around the property border and Marisa listened to her describe the changes she wanted to get made.

Marisa liked the idea of having most of the parking lot replaced with grass and a flower garden. She was surprised when Alex said that the parking in front of the building would be assigned by office location. That meant her parking space would be the closest to the front door and Alex's would be the farthest from the front door. This surprised her but she kept quiet.

They were just ready to enter when two young ladies arrived. She was introduced to Linda and Lorie the two junior partners whose offices would be next to the entrance area.

They all entered and Marisa walked the hallway listening to what Alex planned to do to the interior. A wider hallway, bigger offices, and top end furniture. She learned that all the offices including her entrance office would have similar furnishing and the interior would have a common theme.

Alex said that the first thing that she needed to get done was to get all the official paperwork masters set up. She asked if Marisa was ready to set up a functioning on the ground office in Evanston, a home office in Cincinnati and one in Oahu, Hawaii.

Marisa smiled and said that she was getting a surprise, after a pleasant surprise, and that she was certainly going to enjoy her new position. She laughed and said that she would need to go to Oahu so that she could properly set up that office.

Linda nodded and said that she and Lorie had an extra room in their apartment where she could stay.

Alex liked the interaction that Marisa was having with the three of them. It spoke well to the atmosphere she wanted to have in the office.

She invited Marissa to join the three of them on a fishing trip the following morning.

Marisa said that she would love to come.

The following morning Matt, Alex, Linda, and Lorie left the house early in the morning and rode the black Jaguar to the harbor. After parking they carried their things to the Golden Goose. A few moments later they watched as Marisa parked her grey Honda and walked up the pier.

Marisa looked at the glistening white yacht with its white canvas cover over the back deck in awe. She had always wanted to go out on such a beautiful boat but had always figured she could not afford to spend that kind of money.

Alex greeted her and said that breakfast was being served and asked Marisa what she wanted with her pancakes.

Marisa sat at the table in the galley and watched as the person who had been introduced as Matt made pancakes and fried eggs. She said that one pancake, one over easy egg and one sausage and a cup of coffee would be great.

Matt looked up to the parking lot and announced that the rest of the group going fishing had arrived and as soon as they were onboard they would all go out.

He asked the new arrivals if they wanted breakfast and let them know that the Golden Goose would be underway as soon as everyone was situated.

The group came on board and one of them said she wanted breakfast but the other four said they had already eaten.

Matt got them situated. He then gave them all safety instructions, had them each put on and adjust their life vests. He then asked them to keep the vests close by but let them know that they did not need to wear them.

He pulled in the boarding ramp and pulled in the lines tying the Golden Goose to the pier. He climbed up to the conning area and maneuvered out of the harbor.

Linda and Lorie shared their memories with Marisa of the last time the two of them had gone out on the Golden Goose.

Marisa said she remembered some of the news reports at that time but none of those reports had any of the details that she was now hearing.

Once he was out to the fishing site, Matt turned off the engine and proceeded to get the five customers that had come on board for the fishing trip fishing. He helped bait their hooks with the bait they chose and if they asked he cast their line.

Alex watched as Linda and Lorie helped Marisa get her pole ready. It turned out that Marisa was a person that loved to fish and didn't need any help. Everyone had their lines ready in short order.

The fishing was good, and everyone was catching fish.

Hawaiian Princesses

Matt was busy making sure the fish were put into the holding tanks where they would stay alive until they were cleaned.

He got the grill going and put on hamburgers, sausages, brats, ears of corn, carrots, and broccoli. Earlier he had made two large coolers filled with tea and lemonade. There were also soft drinks, beer, and wine in the refrigerator.

He made a point of letting everyone know that it was all you could eat, and drink and lunch would be available from ten thirty to noon.

Lorie was fishing near Marisa and telling her Alex stories.

Marisa learned how Alex had rescued the two of them and their mother from the forest of Pennsylvania and while doing so had been shot by the man who was their father, and that Alex had shot and killed him. She went on to share how the person that both she and Linda thought of as their aunt had also launched their mother's art career and later on a vacation to Hawaii their mother had met the person who she her fell in love with and who the two of them now considered to be their father.

After catching three nice bass, Marisas decided that she would have a glass of wine, sit under the canopy, enjoy the view, and watch the other people fish.

Alex joined her with a glass of lemonade and asked if she was enjoying herself.

Marisa said that she was and that she had learned a ton about the person she was now working for.

Alex smiled and said that she was sure that Lorie had embellished the stories she had heard.

Marisa shook her head and said that if even half of it was true it was still an amazing story. She thanked Alex for inviting her out fishing and said that doing something like this had always been on her bucket list.

Alex said she was happy to have helped get it checked off. She then invited Marisa to a dinner of freshly caught fish at her house.

When they returned to the peer, Alex led the way to the fish cleaning station and said that everyone cleaned the fish they had caught. She was quickly done with the three fish she had caught and then helped Linda and Lorie clean theirs.

It was clear that Marisa was a fisherman because she had her three cleaned in record time and then cleaned one of Lorie's.

Lorie and Linda had each caught five large trout.

It was early afternoon and they all agreed to go to the house, shower and then spend some time by the pool.

Marisa said she would go home, take a shower, and then come over and join them at poolside.

Alex made sure that Marisa took an extra fish home because Linda and Lorie were leaving the next day, and it would be only her and Matt at the house for a few days.

<u>Chapter 6: Parent Plot</u>

Rose-Anne and Brian were exchanging experience stories over dinner at his house. Annie had invited them for a poolside dinner. The sun was slowly making its way down a dark blue sky toward the horizon and would soon disappear just off the tip of Lanai. It was a moment of quiet where everyone was in an observation mode and locked into thoughts of their own.

Brian's thoughts took him back to Pukalani where he had grown up. He had watched similar sunsets from a very young age and had many wonderful memories of growing up with his adopted parents. Pukalani was a home that had been and was still full of love where his adopted parents took care of children while their parents worked.

Annie's thoughts took her back to the forests of Pennsylvania where she had spent fifteen years chained by her ankle to a post in the center of a cabin and where she had given birth to Linda and Lorie. The sunset, though splendorous, raised memories that she would rather not have thought of.

They were memories of years of trying to keep from going insane. Painting had provided the basis for keeping her sanity.

Rose-Anne thought of the many sunrises that she, Russel and Alex had enjoyed out on Lake Michigan when they went fishing. The golden sunset brought a warmth to her heart that made her a little melancholy. She watched Aurea's face and wondered what was in her mind. She hoped to see that her mind was developed and would be filled with great memories.

Aurea was drawn to the beauty of the dark ocean water that contrasted against the lighter blue of a cloudless sky with the sun slowly turning from its bright yellow to a richer lustrous orange as it slipped below the far horizon. She thought briefly of her birth parents and then of Alex and Matt, who were now the two she thought of on a daily basis and who she loved. She was sad by having lost her birth parents, but she felt blessed to have been put on the porch of Alex and Matt.

Russel had his arm around Rose-Anne and thought how far he had come from the single room shack in Mississippi to the house where they had raised Alex. He thought of the fishing trips, helping Alex with her homework, becoming a professor, and gaining a position where he had now been teaching for more than thirty-five years.

He was holding Aurea's hand and could feel her squeeze it as the sun got close to the horizon and he wondered what was going through her mind.

Aurea knew that she was in a new wonderous world with people that had warm hearts and who didn't know how rich they were. They were rich in friendship, and they were rich in the caring they shared and finally they were rich in the things they owned. She was especially happy that they were rich in the love they gave her.

She squeezed her new grandfather's hand and thought about her new mother.

The sun set and they all turned their attention to the Hawaiian centered dinner.

Rose-Anne had prepared Poke using cubed fresh ahi tuna combined with onions, red Limu kohu seaweed, all sprinkled with sesame seeds and sprinkled with soy sauce.

Anne had prepared a side dish of Lomi Lomi Salmon which she had prepared in the traditional Hawaiian way using massaged salted salmon mixed with onions, tomatoes, and a touch of hot peppers.

Brian had prepared Kulua pork that he had cooked in his underground oven known as an imu. He was proud of the family recipe. He had also cooked the rice on which the Kulua pork was served and the wedge of cabbage that went with it. He enjoyed Aurea's comment that it was the best pork she had ever tasted. She also said that she loved the sweet bean and sweet potato filled manapua buns.

When she tried the creamy, cooled haupia pudding she smiled and said that the entire dinner had been super, but the rich coconut flavored pudding was the best desert she had ever tasted.

Everyone was flush with the good food they had eaten, the table was cleared, and they all sat down to enjoy an evening of conversation, a good glass of wine or in Aurea's case a cherry coke.

The conversation turned to Alex's new venture and the fact that Linda and Lorie were both now junior partners with her.

Rose-Anne said that she was pleased that Alex had chosen to come and live with her and Russel. She gave Aurea a hug and said that she was looking forward to teaching Aurea the thrill of the kitchen.

Aurea laughed and said that she was looking forward to going fishing with her father and grandfather out on the lake each weekend, in learning to ice skate and making new friends at school.

Brian said that he and Kekoa had identified three potential cases that would help get the investigative business launched. It would be their gift to Linda and Lorie so they could earn their stripes and help the business at the same time.

Rose-Anne said that she had several potential cases, but they were not necessarily of financial benefit since many of her cases were pro bono. Her biggest concern was that her daughter was constantly in gun battles that somehow she survived but the move to Evanston meant that she did not have the partner that had been her backup in Cincinnati.

Brian shared how Alex had worked with some Hawaiian detectives and had arranged to have the backup she needed when she solved the Pool of Blood case.

Aurea had been listening and asked where the pool of blood was located.

Brian smile and said that it was at the base of one of the waterfalls on the road to Hannah and if she wanted to go there he would take her there so she could see how beautiful it was.

Aurea said she probably had seen the waterfall, but she had not heard the story that went with it.

Rose-Anne said that visiting that waterfall and hearing about the story that went with it would be a great way to spend their last day on Maui.

Brian let them know that Linda and Lorie were on the way back and he would invite them to join them for this last day and they could share the story of their fishing trip out on the Golden Goose.

They all agreed to a late breakfast the next day and the dinner broke up.

The next day, Linda and Lorie were a surprise at breakfast. They had flown in when they had learned it was the last full day that Aurea was going to be in Maui. They said that they wanted to be there and make sure she had a great day.

Aurea enjoyed the attention and said that she was looking forward to the day and finding out more about what her mother had done on the Island.

Annie said that her mother was very well known among law enforcement for solving a case where a serial killer had operated just below the radar and killed more than sixteen people over as many years. She had given much of the credit to three local detectives that ended up being promoted and were now living on Oahu.

Lorie said that she and Linda had made contact with those three and would be doing lunch with them in the near future.

As the Breakfast ended Brian suggested that they take two cars out to the falls where Alex had captured and subsequently killed the serial killer.

Aurea chose to ride with Linda and Lorie who said they had a convertible.

The ride took them to the other side of the Island and out on the road to Hannah. At the third waterfall they stopped and parked.

Brian led the way to a spot near the pool at the base of the twin streams of the waterfall. He pointed to the right stream and said that was the spot where the serial killer slit the victim's throat and after the blood had been wash into the pool below, he would jump down and swim in the "Pool of Blood."

He then led the way up the path to the spot where Alex had stood and confronted the killer as he was about to cut the throat of his next victim. He hid behind the victim and peeked around her head. He threatened to slice her throat, and Alex shot him through the one eye that was visible. He dropped the knife staggered backward and fell to the pool below. The young lady was traumatized but she recovered and was now a member of the Maui police department. She credited Alex with changing her life and giving her a purpose that she had never had before.

Aurea went to the edge of the stone in the middle of the two streams and looked down at the pool below. She said that it was a long way down and she would not have jumped down, so the killer was at least crazy enough to not be afraid of the jump. She looked at the spot where the victims were made to stand, then after a moment she asked where the killer had taken the bodies so he would not be discovered.

Brian smiled and said that she was going to make a good detective someday. He pointed up the trail and said there was a ravine not far up the trail where all the bodies were found. It was the place that Alex had predicted they would find the bodies. He said that she had nailed every detail of the case with the help of Johnnie, who she called her magician.

Aurea smiled and said that his wife, Mary, was the person who had helped her after she lost her parents, to make the transition to her new world and added that if he was a magician, she was a loving sorcerous.

Annie gave her a hug and said that everyone around her mother loved her and that she was in very good hands.

Aurea nodded and said that the parents she had at birth and the parents she had now had all shown her how much they loved her. She said that she was very lucky and then she looked at Lorie and asked where they were going to have lunch and did anyone want to go windsurfing.

Linda named the restaurant on the way back that had a deck that looked out over the area where the wind surfing was done. She suggested they go there for lunch and then go wind surfing.

Kekoa and Anela joined them and during the discussion over lunch he shared a potential case of a wayward billionaire in the Chicago area that ran a prostitution ring in the guise of an escort service. He said that she was well connected with the local mafia so it might be a dangerous case, but it would be very rewarding because there was a large amount of money offshore.

Linda and Lorie thanked him and their dad for helping get their new business off the ground. She said that she was sure that Alex would appreciate having an up-front influx of money to get the business on solid ground.

Brian then added that the plane he leased was available to them at any time they needed it. He wanted the two of them to be able to participate fully in the startup of Evercrest, McGregor, Smith, and O'Neill.

Linda looked at Lorie and then asked when he had learned of the name.

He pulled out his phone and showed her the text that he had just received from Alex.

Linda and Lorie took out their phone and received a similar message that explained that Alex had been able to get her long-time partners Trey and Johnnie to join the partnership as two senior partners she had been hoping to have. She added that the next time they were all together for the first time they would all celebrate together on the Golden Goose.

Lorie shook her head and said that she would need to get use to the speed of her new boss.

Linda laughed and said that they were partners with a person who took things on at full speed and seemed to excel in doing so. The two of them would need to take their game to a new level so they could keep up.

Aurea took a sip of her lemonade and said that they should plan for a marathon because her mother had told her that was the way to seem fast while maintaining the energy to keep going.

Lorie gave her a hug and said that it was time to put the thought of work aside and go out and do some windsurfing.

While Linda, Lorie, Aurea and Kekoa went wind surfing, the rest of the group walked along the beach and discussed the new investigative business that Alex was setting up.

Annie said that she was impressed with the fact that a requirement for Linda and Lorie to be named as junior partners had been the fact that they had to paint a picture after every case that they participated in. It made her extremely happy because it would let her see if they could paint well enough to make a living as artists. This would give them an out if being an investigator did not provide the fulfillment they hoped it would.

Mary-Anne smiled and added that it sounded like something that Alex would do. She had graduated from Northwestern at the top of her class and had received many offers to work for very prestigious law firms. She had come to work in her office as a junior partner and not long after had left to become a deputy in a small town just to the northwest of Evanston for a fraction of the salary that she was making. She added that at that time she thought Alex was crazy but now it was clear that she had made the choice that most attracted and enticed her. She added that Alex had let her know it was not about money, but it was about having passion for the work that she did.

Annie nodded and said that Alex had pushed her to accept her passion for painting and to have the confidence that her paintings were great. She added that Alex had not waited for her to realize that but had pushed her and had recruited the person who was now her partner by showing her some of the paintings and getting the hundreds of paintings displayed and put on sale. She had pulled her from being chained in the forest to being a world recognized painter in less than two years. And it was on a vacation to Maui that Alex had insisted she come on that she had met Brian. She added that she credited Alex as having changed her world.

<u>Chapter 7: The Flight of the Lieutenant</u>

The next day, Linda, Lorie, Mary-Anne, Russel, and Aurea boarded the private jet and flew to Oahu. Linda and Lorie got out and a few moments later they watched as the plane taxied out for takeoff on the way to Evanston, Illinois. Linda commented that it had been a great visit to Maui. They then took a taxi to their apartment and walked in to find a pile of moving boxes in each of the rooms. They were happy that the furniture had been delivered and put in place before their boxes had arrived this at least gave them a chance to unpack into the right space. They began opening the boxes and were putting things away when Linda got a call.

She said hello, then said that she would be glad to listen to the details.

Lorie listened as arrangements for the person calling to come over to the apartment were made.

After the call ended they went into the bedroom that was to be their office. They were glad that the only thing they had to deal with were the office supplies. They put them all into one of the cabinets then went into the kitchen and got an assortment of drinks, went back to their office, and put everything into the small refrigerator sitting on top of a double cabinet credenza. They looked around and agreed that it was presentable though it still needed have a few pictures hung and something put on the meeting table.

They moved all the boxes that were in the way of someone getting to the room and then sat down to recover from their frantic pace.

Lorie sent a message to Alex saying that they had a client coming over and they had none of the paperwork that they needed to get the client to sign a contract or for them to agree to non-disclosures.

She got a check mark back and then a slew of documents were sent to her e-mail. She got on the office computer that was to be hers and fired it up. The documents came through her email. She printed off a few of each of the ones she thought they would need and arranged them on her desk.

She showed Linda the documents and pointed to the letter head that read, ***Evercrest, McGregor, Smith & O'Neill Partners, LLC***. She said that they now knew that Alex had been able to recruit her long-term partner and her magician to join the practice. She added that they were lucky to have gotten in as junior partners.

A few moments later, the doorbell rang. The lady at the door was in a Navy uniform. She introduced herself as Lieutenant Lydia Murray.

Linda and Lorei shook her hand and led her to the bedroom office. They were glad that this bedroom, meant to be the master bedroom had a great view of the marina and all the boats anchored there.

Lydia looked out at the harbor commented about the great view then looked around the room and said that it looked like they were just moving in.

Linda said that they had arrived that morning from Maui, and it was their first day in the apartment. She added they had hurriedly straightened out the office before her arrival and that the office was mostly empty but there were soft drinks in the refrigerator.

Lydia thanked her and said that for the moment she was fine.

She then said that what she was going to share with them needed to be confidential.

Lorie put one of the confidentiality documents on the table and said that they should all sign it to ensure everything was legal. She clarified the fact that as private investigators the confidentiality agreement would not allow them to withhold information if what they were investigating was a part of a criminal investigation by the police.

Lydia nodded and signed.

Linda and Lorie signed below her signature.

She stated that she believed a fellow officer was committing rape and might even have killed one of the young women he raped.

She shared the fact that a civilian friend was missing and the last she had seen of her was the previous Friday night when she was dancing with the Lieutenant. She had observed them leaving together later in the evening.

She had tried calling her friend the next morning but could not reach her by phone. She had gone to her friend's apartment to see if she was there. After convincing the building manager to let her in she found the place empty. She checked to see if her friend had changed out of the clothes that she had worn on Friday night and found none of that in the clothes hamper or in the closet. This was what caused her to think that foul play might be the cause.

She returned to the base where she had asked Lieutenant Halloway if he knew where her friend might be. He said that they had gone for a scenic boat ride and then afterwards he had gone to his officers' quarters, and the young lady he was with had taken a taxi.

She looked at Linda and then at Lorie and said that she was coming to them for two reasons. She had seen their advertisement and had looked up the name O'Neill and had found what she thought was their father's name and had read about several cases that he had solved. She asked if Brian O'Neill was their father.

Linda nodded and said that he was.

The other reason I chose to come to you was that you described yourselves as two female detectives that solved tough cases.

Lorie smiled and then admitted that the two of them were greenhorns, but they were dead shots on the target range, and they were looking to solve the cases that others could not.

Linda pointed to the letter head and added that the Evercrest in the letter head was the most talented female detective in the country and she was the person who had solved the most difficult cases that had stumped other investigators. The McGregor was her long-time partner, and the Smith was the person referred to as the magician because of his internet capabilities. She pointed to O'Neill and said that the two of them were junior partners.

Lorie added that they planned to be as good as Alex Evercrest. She asked if that changed her mind about getting them on her case.

Lydia shook her head and said that she liked the open way the two of them were presenting themselves. She then asked if they wanted to attend the Friday night event at the officer's club that was open to civilians.

Linda said they would certainly be there to observe what was happening.

Linda asked if Lydia could check the with the gate to see if a cab had exited with her friend at the time that she should have left the base.

Lorie asked if Lydia could provide them with a boat with which they could follow Lieutenant Haloway if he went out with some young lady on Friday night.

Linda added that they would like to take it out beforehand and make sure they knew how to handle it because they would most likely be taking it out at night.

Lydia said that if they met her at the gate at nine the following morning she would arrange for them to have a speedboat available and she would rent it for a couple of days. They could also talk with the gate guards about the taxi.

After Lydia left, Lorie suggested they go out and buy some night vision gear so they could keep track of the speedboat the Lieutenant would be using.

Linda suggested they split up, she would continue unpacking stuff and Lorie would go out and find the night vision equipment.

Lorie went to a local hunting outlet and found a 3D Head-mounted Waterproof Night Vision Binocular. She also bought a small professional drone with camera capability. She then purchased a bull horn. She spent under five hundred dollars and felt good about what she had purchased.

She returned to the apartment and showed her purchases to Linda. She said that during the evening they could go out where the boats were docked and practice with both of their new toys. She said that she would see if she could use the drone and camera so they could record what they saw.

The next morning, they met Lydia at the base gate. They inquired about exiting taxis two nights before and found out that there had been none during the time frame that Lydia inquired about.

As they went to where the boat that they would use was tied off, Linda said that it was looking ominous about the fate of her friend.

Lydia said that she hoped she was wrong, but she did not feel good about the situation.

They all went out on the boat and Linda got use to handling it.

Lorie practiced flying her camera drone.

Lydia commented that Lorie was very good with the drone and wondered how long she had been flying it.

Lorie admitted to having purchased it the day before but she owned a small drone that had been her toy when she was younger.

They came back in and tied off the boat and put their equipment into the storage compartment under the back seat.

They agreed to meet at eight that evening at the officers club and then they left.

They called Alex and talked to her about the case and the fact that they were not sure how to charge for their services.

Alex told them to see how the case turned out. She would have Johnnie check on the Lieutenant's finances. She shared that they each would be charged out at four hundred dollars for each chargeable hour.

She then let them know that she was swearing them in as deputies working for her in Hawaii. After the swearing in she reminded them to wear their protective gear and to err on the side of safety. She had Marisa send images of their badges over the phone and let them know that real badges would be delivered to their apartment in the next couple of weeks.

The call reminded Alex that she needed to order a couple of camera drones. She was sure that Johnnie would want a replacement for his drone, Gunjfor, that had been left with the Cincinnati detective department.

Lorie said that she was going to wear a suit style outfit so she could also carry her weapon.

Linda reminded her that they would not be allowed to carry their weapons onto the base.

Lorie smiled and said that then she was going to wear her shorts and high heel outfit and see if she could attract some senior Navy officer.

Linda quipped back that she would need to hide her knobby knees.

The two of them both wore pants suit outfits that would facilitated riding in a speed boat if necessary.

Lydia met them as they came into the officer's clubhouse. They sat together in one of the corner tables. All three of them were drinking non-alcoholic drinks.

They were asked to dance several times, and they took turns keeping track of the Lieutenant who had zeroed in on, had been dancing and sitting with one very attractive young lady with blue eyes, long blond hair, wearing a low-cut dress with both sides of her skirt slit up to her thighs. It was clear to them that she was flirting heavily with the Lieutenant.

They watched as the two of them walked out of the club. He had his arm around her shoulders, and they were laughing as they got to the door.

The three of them got up and followed.

The Lieutenant led the way to the dock.

The three of them went to where their boat was tied off and got into the boat.

Linda started the engine while Lorie got her night vision equipment out and got her drone ready to fly.

They watched as the light on the corner of the Lieutenants boat headed out of the harbor.

Lorie put their light on the floor of their boat so they would not be visible as they followed.

It was a twenty-minute-high speed run out into the ocean before the Lieutenant's boat stopped.

Lorie took her drone in as close as she dared and captured what was going on. The camera caught the Lieutenant roughly stripping the dress off the young woman who began to fight with him. She suddenly she turned and jumped from the boat into the water. The Lieutenant cursed, threw her dress in after her, took a paddle and struct her several times and wished her luck in swimming in. He fired up the boat's engine and headed back to the harbor. He laughed to himself and he thought about the rule that he operated under the rule that if the woman cooperated she got to go back to shore. If she fought him she got to go out to sea.

Linda used the bull horn and told the Lieutenant to stop because he was under arrest.

Lorie caught him giving them the finger as he sped away.

Linda took the boat over to where the young lady was paddling in the water. She was bleeding from the forehead and crying.

Lydia helped Lorie get the young lady into the boat and they headed back toward the harbor.

When they got to shore Lydia said that she would take care of the young lady, and they should go after Lieutenant Haloway.

Linda and Lorie headed to the officers club to make sure the Lieutenant was not there and then went to his address and found that he was not there.

They called Lydia and asked her if she could help them determine where the Lieutenant might have gone.

Lydia said she would check with the gates to see if he had gone out. She called back a few moments later and said that she had tracked him down to a Navy cargo plane that had just taken off and was headed to Naval Base Coronado in California.

Linda asked how fast the cargo plane could fly and learned that it was one of the older turbo prop cargo planes that would take about eight hours to get there.

She called Darrel the pilot of the jet that her father leased and asked if he could leave immediately and fly her to the San Diego International Airport.

Darrel asked what was up.

Linda shared that they were trying to get ahead of a fugitive that was trying to avoid being arrested by flying to the mainland. She clarified that she and Lorie needed to get there ahead of him and arrest him when he landed.

Darrel said he could pick them up at the airport in forty-five minutes and then it would be a five-hour flight to San Diego. He asked if that would put them ahead of the other plane flying there.

Linda said that it would put them there almost two hours ahead of the cargo plane flying there.

Lorie asked Lydia if she could accompany them and if necessary run interference with the Navy brass.

Lydia smiled and asked if she got a commission for being part of the arresting team.

Lorie laughed and said that they had not yet figured out how to make any money on the case, so she was welcome to one hundred percent commission on zero income.

Lydia said that zero was OK as long as they nailed the Lieutenant.

They all went to the private plane parking area at the Daniel K. Inouye International Airport in Oahu to wait for Darrel.

They waited just fifteen minutes before they saw the white jet with the black stripe down its side pull to a stop. Darrel stepped out and greeted them. He asked if they had any luggage.

All of them showed him a small carry on that they said contained their one-day necessities and one change of clothes.

Once they were all on board and taxing out for takeoff, Lorie made a call to Alex.

Alex was still at home having breakfast with her mother and Aurea. She was surprised when she heard what Lorie was sharing with her. She said that she was going to swear them in as deputies in the State of California and would send out their badges to their emails and phones. She asked if there was anyone with them that could act as a witness to their swearing in.

Lorie said that there was a Navy Lieutenant that could be the witness.

Once the swearing in was over, Alex asked if they had their protective gear with them.

Lorie said that they both had their protective gear with them.

Alex wished them luck and said she wanted to hear from them after the arrest.

Once the call was over, Lydia gave a small laugh and said that she felt like she was part of a commissioning team getting a new ship launched.

Linda nodded and said that they had shared the fact that they were just starting up their investigative services. Things were moving much faster than either of them had expected. They had become official deputies it two states two years sooner than they had anticipated and were chasing a fugitive long before they had thought they would be assigned by the business to do so.

Lorie suggested they all get a nap and be ready for what was coming up.

Lydia made a couple of calls and then shared the fact that she knew a Navy Captain at the base who had agreed to meet them at the Naval base gate and escort them to the airfield where the flight would be coming in. She asked whether they thought they needed the military police to be present.

Lorie asked whether the Navy would charge the Lieutenant with attempted rape or whether it would be better to arrest him and take him to a civilian court in Oahu.

Lydia thought for a moment and said that she was not sure how the Navy would handle it but suggested they start by taking him to a court outside of the Navy and let the Navy take the action that they thought was appropriate.

They all woke up as the plane touched down in San Diego.

They drove directly to the Naval Base where they were met by Lydia's Captain friend.

He introduced himself as Captain Kirkpatrick and let them know that the flight they were interested in was an hour and a half away. He asked if they might want something for breakfast. He pointed to his car and said that he knew of a place just a few minutes away that had a great menu.

Linda thanked him and said that she was ready for a good breakfast.

During the breakfast it became apparent that Lydia's Captain friend was more than a friend. The two of them admitted that they were in a serious relationship and had notified their commands of the situation.

The Captain got a call and let them all know that the plane was on its approach to land, and they should go out to where it was to be offloaded.

The four of them stood outside of the captains car and watched the plane come in, taxi to its designated area, shut its engines off and get tied down.

Linda and Lorie suggested that they be at the bottom of the steps when Lieutenant Halloway exited the plane.

The Lieutenant came out of the plane and Linda declared that he was under arrest for the attempted murder of the date he had at the Friday night Officer's Club Ladies night event.

Without hesitation, the Lieutenant pulled his weapon and shot Lorie in the chest and was turning to shoot Linda.

She stepped in towards him, grabbed his gun wrist and pointed it down at his foot. The movement fired his second shot that went into his foot. She then put her finger on top of his and pointed the gun at his left knee and pulled the trigger.

The Lieutenant screamed after each shot. He let the gun fall from his hand and fell to the ground and lay on his back moaning.

Linda kicked his gun away, grabbed his wrist and twisted it causing him to roll over. She grabbed his other wrist and handcuffed him with his hands behind his back while he cursed and moaned.

She then pivoted and ran to where Lorie was laying on the ground.

The Lieutenant was now cursing and threatening to kill all of them if he got the chance.

Lorie said that she was going to have a bruise in the middle of her stomach and one on her butt from having landed so hard, but she was going to be fine.

Linda heard the Captain calling in the shooting and asking for the shore patrol, and two ambulances.

Withing minutes the area was a sea of shore patrol personnel, an EMT vehicle and the siren and lights of the ambulance could be heard.

As Linda looked around she realized that the military vehicles did not have the same look as those in the civilian world but the men and women all acted the same.

Lorie got a field inspection and then was put in an ambulance and whisked away.

Another ambulance arrived and the Lieutenant was put in it and taken away.

Linda made sure that the Lieutenant would be put under guard because he was under arrest and would be taken back to Oahu to face murder, attempted murder and fleeing the scene of a crime.

She was asked by one of the MP's if she was armed and had used her weapon. She said she was armed but had not used her weapon. She used her phone to show her badges valid in both California and Hawaii.

Captain Quinly vouched for her and said that he would ensure that she was available for any follow-up that might be required.

The plane was allowed to unload. The crew went through a questioning session and then was told that they would be allowed to return to Oahu once all the reports were written.

It was close to noon before Linda was allowed to leave with Lydia and the Captain.

Lydia commented that she had not expected the Lieutenant to try to kill them.

Linda said that she had been surprised and was a bit shaken. She had never shot anyone, and she was not sure how she felt.

Lydia said that she had a great therapist back on Oahu who she could recommend.

They arrived at the base hospital and went in.

Lorie was in an observation room in the emergency area. They entered and she said that she had arrived and had been given a CT scan to make sure there was no internal damage, and she was now waiting for the doctor.

Linda decided that it was a good time to give Alex a call and let her know what had happened. She excused herself and said she was going to take a walk.

When Alex received the call she was in a discussion with the contractor that was doing the remodeling of the interior of the building that she had just purchased.

Trey, Johnnie, and Marisa were at the reception entrance area discussing how they would be working together.

Alex went up to where they were sitting and put her phone in speaker mode and asked Linda to describe what had happened.

Trey commented that it seemed odd that the Lieutenant had acted so violently. He added that perhaps Linda should see if there was more going on than just his flight from the attempted drowning of his victim. He asked if they had checked on his other duties and if there might be some sort of other activity going on.

Linda thanked him for the suggestion because it had not occurred to her.

Johnnie said he would see if he could find some sort of money trail.

Linda added that the Kevlar vest had saved Lorie and that it would be hard for them to leave their apartment without wearing it.

Alex commended them on wearing their protective gear, then she reminded Linda that she and Lorie were on the hook to paint something about the case that they were on the verge to solving. She asked if the shooting scene might be a good subject for the painting.

Linda hung up and sat down on a bench along the walk. She made a call to her mother.

Annie was just finishing putting her breakfast dishes into the dishwasher. She listened to what had happened and mentally thanked Alex for having insisted on the use of the bulletproof vests. She was surprised that it had stopped a 405 bullet at a three-foot distance. She had tears in her eyes as she listened to Linda. Once again she wished the two of them had become artists instead of following Alex and Brian into being crime investigators.

Linda ended the conversation saying that she was now on the hook to paint a picture, and she was going to discuss that with Lorie over lunch.

Annie smiled and again thanked Alex.

Ron Mueller

<u>Chapter 8: The Lieutenant's Network</u>

On the flight back to Oahu, the three of them discussed how to close the case. Lorie suggested that they go out to where they had rescued the young lady on Friday night and determine the direction of the sea current and measure how fast it moved. They then could calculate how far a body might have drifted. Then they could get the coast guard to go out and look for the body that they all agreed was somewhere out at sea.

Linda said that it was a great idea and it might be enough to convince the Coast Guard to go out for a look.

Lydia shook her head and said it was hard for her to accept the fact that her friend had been killed. She found it hard to think that going out on a Friday night could end so horribly.

Linda nodded and agreed. She said that she would like to use the speed boat that they had used one more time when they got back to the island. She added that they were getting some additional help in finding out what else the Lieutenant might have been doing.

Lydia shared the fact that her Captain had agreed to have the Lieutenant flown back to Maui. He would be kept in the hospital under guard until he could be moved to the brig.

They landed in the late afternoon and decided to go to dinner then call it a day and get a good night's sleep.

The next morning, they met Lydia at the entrance gate. She had a Coast guard officer, Captain Saure, with her. He said that he was interested in how they were determining where a body might be found before he was ready to deploy one of the coast guard vessels out to see if they could find it.

They all went to the dock where the boat was tied off and went out.

Lorie was the one that had kept track of the location. She guided them to the spot where they had rescued the young woman.

She launched her small drone and set it up to maintain an exact position.

Then they measured the direction and the speed that a small flat piece of wood floated away from that fixed position. After an hour of following the drifting wood they had the information that was needed.

Lorie spent a few moments on her computer calculating the distance then asked Captain Saure for his email address and sent him the coordinates of where the coast guard should find the body of a young woman.

He said that he was impressed with how they had made the measurements and he was now confident enough to send out a vessel in search of a body. He warned them that they would still be very lucky to find a body out at sea

When they returned to the pier, Lydia asked about lunch.

Lorie reminded Linda that they had scheduled a lunch with David, Malia, and Leilani the detectives from Maui that had been promoted when the Pool of Blood case was solved.

They made arrangements with Lydia for lunch on the upcoming Friday.

The lunch with the three turned out to be both pleasant and very helpful. Leilani said that she and her team would look into the missing person's reports to see if any corresponded with the Friday night officer club invitationals. She also suggested a judge and said she would see about getting her on the case. Finally, she gave Linda the name of a lawyer that she might want to utilize.

Lorie thanked the three and said that she and Linda would keep them informed about the case and they would be pleased to give them weekly updates.

Lieutenant Halloway was flown back to the Oahu Naval base where he was formally arrested and kept under guard..

He then found a lawyer to represent him and vowed to sue Linda for having shot him.

Linda consulted with Alex and got her agreement to utilizing both the recommended judge and to retain the lawyer. She closed with saying she would report any significant information as it occurred.

Lorie shared the fact that her huge purple bruise was beginning to turn a putrid yellowish and grey and the pain was down to a mere mosquito size or maybe a mole hill.

Alex laughed and said she was well aware of the cycle of pain after having been shot and hoped that Lorie would not be surprised next time.

Johnnie came on and said that he was sure that there had to be more people involved in a redirection of government equipment, weapons, and munitions because he had found an offshore bank account that had three billion dollars in it under the Lieutenant's name.

Trey came on and suggested that there had to be a person on the Oahu end, another on the airplane, and at least another at the San Diego base. He suggested that they find out all the sites where the cargo plane flew and check those locations out for missing shipments.

After the call they decided to confront the Lieutenant to see if they could get any more information from him.

Before they got there they got a call from Leilani letting them know that there were at least three more women who had attended the Friday night officer's club gathering that had been on the missing person's list.

Linda looked at Lorie, shook her head, and said, "the Lieutenant seems to be a serial rapist and killer."

When they entered the hospital room he cursed them for having put him in the hospital.

Lorie replied that he had shot her, and he was lucky to be alive because she had not been able to shoot back.

Linda smiled and said the she had read the report about the incident and the only gun that had been fired was his and the only fingerprints on the gun were also his. That meant he had shot himself in the foot and in his right knee. It was going to be impossible for him to put the blame on either of them. In fact, he was being charged with an attempt to kill a law enforcement officer, an attempt to drown his Friday night date and fleeing the secene of a crime. She then asked how many other women had he left out at sea?

He shook his head and quit talking.

She stopped for a moment and then said that they were now following up on his smuggling ring.

The Lieutenant remained silent. Then he smiled and commented that he thought they were just fishing.

Lorie smiled and gave him the name of his offshore bank and the fact that he had three billion dollars in an account under his name there. She asked him how he had accumulated such a grand sum of money on the salary of a Lieutenant.

Linda followed up by asking him to name the people working with him.

The Lieutenant shook his head and asked if there was any possibility that he could make a deal with them for a significant part of the money.

Linda smiled and asked if he had paid taxes on the money in the bank.

He shook his head and asked if she were kidding.

Lorie explained that if he had not, she and Linda would likely get a thirty percent finders reward from the IRS.

Linda asked if he wanted to give them the rest to put into charity work.

The Lieutenant was silent for a moment and asked what they wanted from him.

Lorie said they wanted the names of the people working with him. If he gave them the names they would work with the district attorney to give him a break on the smuggling part of the charges he would be facing and ask for only fifteen years with the possibility of parole.

He looked at her and said that he would be an old man by that time.

Linda then added that if they did not get the names of his accomplices they would make sure he got thirty years in prison. She then put her phone on record and asked him for the names of his accomplices and their rank and their locations.

He replied that he would give her the names if she gave him a signed document that described the deal that they were offering.

Linda nodded and said that they would be back as soon as they had that agreement in writing.

Lorie said it might be a good idea to see if Leilani could introduce them to the prosecutor that would be handling the Lieutenant's case and discuss the deal that they were discussing.

Leilani agreed and set up a meeting that day over lunch.

Linda thanked her for arranging the meeting so quickly and said that she would cover the cost of lunch.

At lunch, Leilani introduced the prosecutor, Kaleo Palakiko who would be the prosecutor.

Linda explained the situation and the fact that they were charging the Lieutenant in civil court instead of the military one because along with the smuggling charges, they were also sure that he would be charged with attempted rape, rape, murder, and possibly multiple murders. They let him know that the Coast Guard was out looking for the body of a young woman that they were sure the lieutenant had murdered.

Leilani added that she had the missing person's reports that they would most likely link to the Lieutenant.

Lorie explained that they were trying to get him to reveal the people involved with the smuggling ring and had made the claim that they could get a deal that would reduce a thirty-year sentence to fifteen years. She clarified that as soon as they had the body that the Coast Guard had gone out to recover, they wanted to add the additional murder charges.

Kaleo laughed, said that he did not want to play poker with them and said that the two of them should work for him. He liked the way they were playing the Lieutenant. He said that he would accompany them on a visit to the Lieutenant, make him the offer and have a signed agreement when he left. He added that he hoped that the Coast Guard would find the body because if they did this preliminary negotiation would mean very little to the Lieutenant because the murder charges would trump the smuggling charges.

The next day the Linda, Lorie and Kaleo entered the Lieutenant's hospital room.

It took only a few minutes for Kaleo to make the agreement and give the Lieutenant a signed agreement.

Linda got the names of the person who arranged the loading and the redirect of the load, and five people who off loaded the redirected items and had them shipped to the addresses that were given to them by the Lieutenant.

They left the hospital and went to meet Lydia for lunch. When they arrived, they were surprised that Captain Saure was with her.

He said that the Coast Guard had found the body almost at the exact spot that they had calculated. He said they were on the way in and wondered if the two of them had made arrangements to have the body examined.

Linda said she was going to make a quick call and stepped outside. She called Leilani and asked if the police coroner would do an autopsy of the body.

Leilani said that she would have the coroner meet the ship, obtain the body, and then do the autopsy. She added that she would inform Kaleo.

When she returned to the table, Lydia let her know that the Navy wanted to take over the smuggling case. She asked if that would an issue.

Lorie smiled and said that it would simplify their lives if that happened but they wanted to continue to handle the rape and murder charges. She added that she figured between the Navy and the civil charges the Lieutenant would go to jail for the rest of his life.

Linda gave Lydia, Kaleo's card and said that they had just extracted the names of the people involved in the smuggling ring and he would work with the navy prosecutors.

After lunch Linda and Lorie discussed what they should do next. Linda replied that they needed to send a detailed report to Alex. Then they needed to get Leilani to work with Kaleo and link the missing person's reports for the three missing young women to the Lieutenant.

Lorie called Kaleo and shared what had transpired at lunch and told him to expect a call from someone in the Navy. She added that he should work with the Navy on the smuggling part but insist that the rape and murder charges were kept in the public domain.

Kaleo replied that he would keep the rape charges in civil court, but he suggested that they turn over the murder charge to the Navy because in that system he would face the death sentence and would very likely try to get that reduced by identifying any other young women he might have killed. He added that the rape charges would be hollow if he charged him with murder and lost.

Lorie thanked him for the information and said that she would discuss it with her boss to see how the firm wanted to handle the matter.

In discussions with Alex, Linda and Lorie agreed that they should hand over the case to the Navy and let the prosecuting Judge Advocate handle the details of the case. She suggested meeting with that person and seeing how they could be of help.

They should work with the IRS to get their reward for finding the money in the offshore bank account. Alex pointed out to them that once the Navy learned of the account they would want that money.

She made the point that the money would come to the Evercrest, McGregor, Smith, and O'Neill Investigation Firm. Each of them and the firm would get one sixth of that money. She asked how the two of them felt about their share that would be fifty million dollars each. She said that the two of them had provided the firm a solid start and that allowed all of them breathing space as they started up.

Alex shared that Johnnie had continued investigating where the smuggled goods ended up and had found one destination where most of the smuggled goods went. The location was in California. He had determined that it was a seemingly legitimate business. It was owned by a holding company that distributed survival supplies around the world. His additional digging identified that the goods went to several individuals that were on the list of gunrunners. The money that was exchanged ended up in overseas accounts in numerous countries.

She added that she wanted the two of them to work with Johnnie and when they had a solid understanding of that part of the smuggling ring they would decide how to handle it. She added that EMSO's objective would be to get their share of the money that Johnnie had found in the offshore accounts.

Chapter 9: Gun Runner Connection

Linda and Lorie got off the call, looked at each other and said that they would need to talk with Johnnie to see if there was something they could do to investigate the company that was receiving the smuggled goods and the person who was in charge of that company.

Lorie called Johnnie to see what they should do next to find the person distributing the stolen Navy goods.

Linda searched for the flight times that would take them to San Francisco where the stolen goods were being handled and distributed.

The two of them had decided that they would reserve using the private jet for situations just like the one they had just used it for or when they were flying all the way to Evenston, Illinois.

Johnnie went into detail of what he had been doing and what he had found.

Lorie was impressed with his ability to hack his way through almost every firewall he encountered. She asked him how he did it and started to learn some of the ways. She got several of his hacking bots and said she was going to learn how to do some of what he was doing.

Johnnie laughed and said that he did not want to corrupt such a young lady. He gave her the company's San Francisco address and the name, Phil Davidson, who was the person he suspected was the kingpin of the distribution operation. He let her know that Phil did not have a police record but was surrounded by armed guards who had a checkered past.

Lorie got off the line with Johnnie and asked Linda if they should go do some on the ground reconnaissance of the company and how they might be carrying out the shipping of the smuggled goods.

Linda said that would be a good idea, but they should clear it with Alex.

In San Francisco, Phil received the bad news. Lt. Halloway had been arrested for murder. He wondered if the smuggling that he was the beneficiary of had been exposed. He decided to step as far back from that operation as possible. He arranged to quickly offload the few remaining goods that he had smuggled from the Navy.

He would need to seek out other connections where he could get the missiles, drones, and ammunition that his customers were so hungry for. He felt sure that he had kept his profile low enough that it would be almost impossible for anyone to connect him to the Lieutenant. He looked at the calendar to see when the next shipment would be loaded. He would make sure that everything associated with the Oahu smuggling operation was part of that shipment. He sent out an order to offload all the goods on the next several shipments.

He had prided himself on keeping his hands clean as he ran his very successful smuggling operation. He had more or less wandered into the business by accident. He had been working very hard at seeking the clothing goods he needed to launch a line he had named "The Angie Davidson Collection" that was named after his mother.

He and she had been very close. She had been a single mother for most of their lives after his father had abandoned them. She had been a great mom who had spent every weekend taking him somewhere fun. He shook his head when he thought about her rapid decline when she had been diagnosed with liver cancer. In less than a year she had gone from a robust fun person to one who was in total misery and could not function by herself. It had been a bitter blessing when she passed away.

The clothing line never materialized because one evening he had been sitting alone when one of the people that he had been doing business with and trying to arrange a shipment of jeans to the US sat down with him and asked if he was interested in making some real money by handling the shipment of goods from the US to various countries around the world.

The conversation took him by surprise, but he listened and figured out how he could actually get into the smuggling business and not get immediately arrested. He was given Lt. Halloway's name as the person to contact. That had been the start of his now very successful operation.

He had studied the situation carefully and had slowly hired his current staff who were ignorant of what they were involved in and were one hundred percent running a legitimate import business. The legitimate business allowed him to run the smuggling operation in its shadow.

He had three enforcers who he had hired from the drug trade, who were aware that they were supporting a smuggling operation. These three were happy to get out of the drug trade because it was safer for them and was just as lucrative.

Lt. Halloway had connected him to the Navy people who were redirecting the smuggled goods. Not long after he got established, numerous gun runners had contacted him, the smuggling operation got up and running smoothly and the money rolled in.

It reminded him of the history of the gold rush where the hard-working miners bought supplies from those providing them and never realized that the suppliers were the ones raking in the big money.

In just a few years he had made billions and was now contemplating getting out of the business. He had kept a low profile and was still driving his old SUV that had more than two hundred thousand miles on its odometer.

The Lieutenants arrest seemed like a warning.

He thought about retirement, but he had expanded his operation and was now connected with weapons suppliers in all of the US military branches. Those connections had come about in an organic fashion. The Navy persons somehow knew someone in the Marine Corps. The Marine Corps person knew someone in the Army and the Army person knew someone in the Airforce. The Airforce person knew of someone in the National Guard. The connection to the Coast Guard had so far not materialized but he figured that the opportunity there was probably as blatant as with the other military branches.

He decided that he needed to get someone to run the current operation and then he could fade into the background and retire to some distant country where he could live like a king.

Johnnie had started his on-line sleuthing at the Lieutenant's bank. He found the link to the offshore account. Once he had hacked into the offshore bank account he was able to find the link to another offshore bank account from where the money was being sent. That account yielded several links from where the money came. There was only one account that was linked to an account that seemed to be an account used for daily personal expenses by the person that seemed to be handling all of them. He focused on learning what he could about the individual, Phil Davidson. He found various businesses owned by the holding company Davidson ran. When he checked out the addresses of the holding companies he suspected that they were empty shell companies that might not even exist in the physical world though they had what seemed like physical addresses. He organized the information he had accumulated and sent it to Alex, Trey, Linda, and Lorie. He hoped that it was in time for them to use it. He had worked through the night; the morning and it was now one in the afternoon which made it eleven in San Francisco.

Alex and Trey had a comfortable flight to San Francisco. They were met by Linda and Lorie as they cleared the customs area. Linda let Alex know that Darrel, the pilot of the private jet leased by her father, would be staying and afterwards they could all fly to the Chicago Executive Airport near Evanston. She and Lorie planned at stay at their apartment there and buy a few things and get settled in before returning to Oahu.

They all drove to the hotel in the same limo. When they arrived, Alex suggested they review how they would proceed.

The four of them checked into the hotel and went into the restaurant and were sitting at a circular booth each sipping on coffee or tea.

They were waiting for a mixed order they jokingly had called their brunch order because for Linda and Lorie it was an early lunch while for Alex and Trey it was more like a late lunch or early dinner when simultaneously all of their phones buzzed. They all said the same word, "Johnnie." Everyone but Alex muted their phone to prevent cross noise contamination. They listened to Johnnie explain that he had found another huge sum of offshore money that if it was seized by the IRS would be even bigger than the one that the Lieutenant had established. He then gave them the name of the person he was sure was the distributor of the smuggled goods. He went on to share the San Francisco addresses that they should check out and the address of the office the distributor, Phil Davidson sat in. He then explained that he had Phil's customer addresses and what he thought were their bank account links but he had not had a chance to verify those connections.

Alex thanked him for his very fast work and suggested that he wait before digging into the customer information until she called him back. She suggested that he go lounge on the Golden Goose, go fishing and enjoy his time until she returned.

Lorie also thanked him and said that she really wanted to learn how he was able to get all the information so quickly. She commented that she thought the name magician did not do him justice and she thought of him as the Grand Internet Wizard.

Johnnie laughed and said that praise was not what he needed. He worked for cookies.

After hanging up Alex explained Johnnies comment about the cookies. They were her reward to him for being her magician.

After their meal, Alex led the way to the car rental booth near the hotel lobby and rented a large black Lincoln sedan.

Lorie signed up as the second driver and volunteered to drive. When they got to the car Trey and Linda got into the back seat. Lorie adjusted the seat and rear-view mirror while Alex plugged in her phone and put in the addresses in the order she wanted to visit them.

The drive to the first address took about five minutes. When they got there Lorie asked if they had the right address as she looked at the post office building.

Linda said she would go in and see if there was a post office box with the suite number Johnnie had given them.

Trey accompanied Linda and a few minutes later they returned. They said that there was a large post office box with the letter designation that Johnnie had given them.

Alex said that she expected the next four would also be P.O. boxes, but they would verify each one.

Lorie drove to each address that turned out to be other post offices.

Two hours later Alex declared the visits over. She suggested they drive by the last address and verify that it was an actual brick and mortar building.

Lorie let out a sigh when they got there and quietly said, "Finally."

Alex declared that their workday was over. She said that she wanted to arrive early the next morning and watch the arrival of the people working there.

Alex suggested that they enjoy one of the Bay area restaurants that had a view of the harbor.

Lorie said that she would be glad to do that. They randomly chose a restaurant and entered. After placing their orders and getting their drinks, Alex asked Linda and Lorie how they felt about the day.

Linda replied that it was somewhat of a letdown, and she had been hoping for something more concrete.

Lorie said that she too was somewhat disappointed.

Alex smiled and said that they should be feeling great. She pointed out that in just one day they had confirmed that a large part of the smuggling organization was a mirage. They had verified that the last address they would visit the following morning was a brick-and-mortar office. She said that the goal the following day was to identify everyone that worked there and to meet Phil Davidson.

She pointed out that Johnnie would do a deep dig into identifying everyone that Phil communicated with. Their job was to talk to as many people as possible and learn what they knew of the operation. This was the gumshoe part of the business that usually led to a break in any case.

She shared that the following day they were all going to be playing the role of business inspectors. She would be the lead inspector and focus on the leader, the organization, and the documentation.

Trey would focus on the safety issues of the environment.

Linda and Lorie would interview the staff and ask what they did and about the work environment.

Their goal was to find out as much as possible about the operation and what each person did.

She pulled out an envelope contained very small, sophisticated bugging devices that Johnnie had sent her out with that would let him get into the phone and wi-fi systems used in the office area.

Linda picked up one of the devices and commented that each of them was paper thin and the diameter of the paper punched out in her three-ring paper punch.

Lorie asked what questions that she and Linda would be asking.

Alex nodded and said that after they enjoyed their meal and took a walk along the waterfront they would gather in the hotel lobby and develop a script with questions for each of them because she needed a script too.

Trey laughed and said that he certainly needed to be given a script for his safety inspection role since he had no clue what that title meant.

Alex said that he was going to be questioning the bodyguards and should keep his cool and not be tempted to shoot any of them as he grilled them.

The meal went by quickly, and they were soon walking along the waterfront. When they got to pier thirty-nine they looked out at all the sea lions lounging on a bevy of platforms.

Lorie looked at the large number gathered on several platforms and wondered if there was a specific reason that the platforms had been provided to host the sea lions.

Trey commented that he had heard their population had greatly expanded and that they hauled out on the platforms to rest and relax. The theory was that they had been given a place to haul out near a place that had plenty of food in the nearby harbor. The platforms provided them a safe place to do so, and it kept them from trying to get onto the many boats tied up along the piers. The sea lions had also become a tourist attraction, so they paid for their place to haul out.

Alex looked out at the large number of sea lions and commented that they seemed to act like a version of their human beach going counter parts, each enjoying themselves in a different way.

She then suggested they get to the hotel and develop their scripts for the following day.

<u>Chapter 10: The Business Inspection</u>

During the writing of the scripts, Alex realized that showing up in a black Lincoln was not the look of an inspection team. She excused herself and said that she was going to rent a plain white van.

She rented the van and then called Marisa and asked her to get magnetic signs made for the van.

Marisa asked if this was a test to see if she had magic powers.

Alex laughed and said it was not but she really needed to get the signs by the following morning.

Marisa called Johnnie to get his help.

He laughed when Marisa explained Alex's request. He was use to Alex's requests. He went online and soon had a sign company that boasted its ability to create any magnetic sign, at any time and have it ready in four hours. He gave that information to Marisa and suggested she call the sign shop and arrange for the signs to be available for pick up in the morning.

Marisa called the number Johnnie had given her.

The person who answered her said he could make the signs she was requesting. He asked what the two foot diameter signs should say.

Marisa replied that she wanted the signs to say, "Evercrest, McGregor, Smith and Obrien Inspectors" and it should be in Script.

The laugh she got stopped her cold. She heard the person on the other end of the phone ask if he could shorten it to "EMSO Inspectors?" If so he could get it done for five hundred per sign plus one thousand dollars for having it ready by ten in the morning.

Marisa said that would be acceptable and then asked if there might be a veterans discount.

She got another laugh and asked who the veteran was and had he seen any combat.

Marisa replied that the veteran was a Trey McGregor who had received a purple heart in Iraq.

There was a moment of silence and then she was told there would be a ten percent discount if he got to meet Mr. McGregor and if he was paid in cash. Marisa said that would be no problem, got the shop owner's name, thanked him, and said that at ten sharp a white van would pull up at his shop.

She hung up and arranged for twenty-five hundred dollars in cash to be sent to the hotel where Alex was staying with instructions to give the money to her. She then called Alex and let her know about the arrangement.

By the time Alex returned the team had finished preparing their scripts that they planned to follow on the next day.

She added that a white van would be available in the morning, and she wanted to get into position early and watch the arrival of the staff. She said that she and Trey would sit in the van and two of them would sit at the bus stop that was just across from the entrance to the office. She asked Linda and Lorie to sit at the bus stop and take a picture of the license plate of each car entering the parking area.

She would park the van so that she could get the picture of each person entering the office. At nine thirty they would all leave to get the signs for the side of the van.

"What time do we leave in the morning," Lorie asked?

"Let's plan leaving at six so we can be in place before people start arriving for work," Alex replied.

She suggested they all retire to their rooms and get a good night's sleep. On the way she stopped at the desk to arrange for the van to be out front at six.

Linda and Lorie went to the elevator together. Lorie commented at the speed that everything was happening and the flexibility that Alex displayed as she thought how to get information. It was a skill the two of them were going to need to develop.

Linda said that it was great to be in the field with Alex and see firsthand how she flexed and adjusted to the situation.

The two of them agreed to get out to the van early.

In the morning, Alex stopped by the desk where she was given an envelope by the receptionist. The note explained that the sign shop wanted to be paid in cash. When she got out to the van she was pleased to see that everyone else was there. She verified that they were all wearing their protective Kevlar vests. Once she had that verified she pointed at the van.

It was much nicer than she had anticipated and had bucket seats for all of them.

Trey volunteered to drive.

Lorie commented that she was not a morning person and right after they left the hotel she was snoozing.

It took about thirty minutes for them to get to the office location.

Linda and Lorie got out of the van and walked about a block to the bus stop across from the office.

Linda commented that the place seemed like any other legitimate business. It was hard to imagine it as the control center of a large smuggling operation.

Alex got out her camera with a large zoom lens and adjusted the settings. She wanted to get pictures of the license plates and pictures of the drivers as they arrived. She immediately noticed that two cars were already parked. She took pictures of the cars and plates and sent them to Johnnie.

Johnnie was set up in his office sipping on a cup of coffee when the pictures of the two cars came in. He immediately ran them through the Chicago DMV computer into which he had hacked. He learned that the older SUV was owned by Phil Davidson and the other vehicle was registered to an Ivan Lubosky who had been arrested for manslaughter, but the charge had been dropped. He sent this information out to Alex and figured that there would soon be additional license plate numbers and pictures.

Phil had arrived early to the office because he was expecting a call from one of his dealers. He had been followed from his home to the office by the three bodyguards that he had hired. He hoped to never need them, but he wanted to have the protection available and on call. He had arranged for them to have the office across from his and had one of them always standing in the hallway in front of his office. He also provided them with a Range Rover that was only two years old while he still drove his more than ten-year-old SUV, and they also had a reserved parking spot next to his car.

A few minutes after eight his support secretary rang in and let him know that the person he was meeting with was on the line. He did not pick up but instead used his phone to establish the call with that person and then hung up the landline. He was negotiating the sale of the last of the Navy armament that had arrived from Oahu.

He was eager to get the set of torpedoes off his hands. He wanted to erase all connection with the Navy smuggling operation.

Not long after out at the bus stop, Linda looked at her watch and saw that it was nine thirty and it seemed that everyone had arrived.

Alex called at exactly that time to get both of them to return to the van.

When they arrived at the sign shop and went in, the owner introduced himself as Arie and asked to shake Trey's hand. He said that he had a tour of Iraq in the infantry and had been part of the initial rush across the desert at the beginning.

Trey said he was pleased to meet him and let him know that he had been in the Marines and had been a sniper. There was a moment of silence as the two stood looking at each other.

Alex broke the moment by inquiring about the sign.

Arie smiled and said that they were done and ready to be put on the side of their van. He commented that a Marisa assured him that he would be paid in cash.

Alex smiled and said that she had the cash.

Arie picked up the two signs and walked out to the van. He expertly put the magnetic signs on, smiled, pointed at the sign, and said, "made and delivered as promised." He looked at them and said they did not seem to be inspectors, but they now had the signage that declared that they were. He led the way back into the store and handed Alex the bill for eighteen hundred dollars.

Alex looked at it and said that he deserved a tip for getting the job done as quickly as he had done it and handed him two thousand dollars in cash.

She led the way to the van and said they were off to inspect the smuggling business and see what they could learn.

When they arrived, Alex led the way in and handed the support secretary the official looking order to do the inspection. She introduced Linda and Lorie as the office inspectors, Trey as the safety inspector and herself as the leadership inspector.

The support asked for them to wait for a moment

Alex watched as the support walked down the hallway to an office that had a person standing across from the door.

Phil had just gotten off the phone when there was a knock on the door. He called out, "come in."

His support explained the situation. He looked at the order to inspect. It looked official and had the embossed seal of the state Environmental Protection Agency on it. He cursed under his breath but figured the easiest way to handle the situation was to get it over with. He knew that they would find nothing out of the ordinary as part of the visit.

He got up and followed his support out to the reception area.

He looked at the four people and was somewhat apprehensive about the situation. They looked too professional and alert to be mere inspectors. He looked over his shoulder and was relieved to see his three guards standing behind him. He wondered if one of the gun runners were trying to make a move.

The thought that the four might also be with law enforcement crossed his mind as well.

He introduced himself and asked why he had not been informed about the inspection.

Alex replied that the inspections were always unannounced so the inspectors would see things as they would normally be.

Phil nodded and asked how long the inspection would take for a simple office area.

Alex explained that it could be as short as an hour unless there were warehouses or production facilities to check. She then introduced Linda and Lorie as the office area examiners, Trey as the safety examiner and herself as the person that would interview him.

Phil nodded and invited her to come to his office. He pointed to his three guards and said that they were his safety team. He then turned and headed for his office.

Trey walked up to the three and introduced himself and asked if there was a good place where they could discuss the safety of the operation. He could tell that the three were not sure what to make of the situation. He figured he would keep asking questions and get them into a discussion of their background.

Alex saw that Linda and Lorie were getting into their script. She followed Phil to his office and sat down. She first asked about his family and how everyone was.

He thanked her for asking but made the point that he had no immediate family.

It was clear to her that he was not going to be friendly about the situation.

Phil asked if she had any proof of who she was.

Alex nodded and said that she was a sheriff in the San Francisco Sheriff's office and served on the inspection division during low level work periods. She pulled out her Sheriff's badge and put it on the table.

Phil's defenses went up immediately. He was impressed with the black woman's confidence, but he sensed that she was there for more than just inspecting the operation. He was right but had no idea what was really happening.

Alex planted her listening device on the underside of the desk. She knew that Johnnie would soon use it to get into the internal internet and then he would be able to get into the phone system and would learn the phone numbers of all the phones.

Linda and Lorie went from office to office interviewing the six persons that comprised the office staff. They planted the listening devices that Alex had given them to plant. The devices were paper thin transparent plastic discs less than a quarter of an inch in size. Once put in place the device became almost invisible.

Linda chose to place her devices where the desk top curled to meet the body of the desk. She was pleased that it was almost invisible, and it could not be felt.

Lorie would pass a business card to the person she was interviewing and in doing so would reach across the desk and place the device on a random object that was out on the desk.

Trey had an easier time since he was standing and walking around the office as he interviewed the three persons in the room with him.

In Phil's office, Alex asked how long he had been in business and asked about the organizational structure.

Phil excused himself for a minute saying that he needed to get a piece of information that Alex had asked for. He went across the hall and asked for Ivan to step out for a minute. Once Ivan was out in the hall, Phil instructed him to follow the inspection van when it left to see where it went. He let him know that he was suspicious about the inspection.

He then went to the desk of his support and asked for the employees records from the beginning until now and it was to include those that had chosen to leave. He observed the two doing the interviews sitting in two separate offices and wondered what they were asking. He smiled as he thought about the fact that the people in the offices were all doing legitimate legal business. He then returned to his office.

Alex had taken the time to move the listening sensor to Phil's side of the desk.

When he returned she was sitting where she had been when he left.

Trey watched as Ivan came back into the room. He sensed that Ivan had been given some sort of instruction. He continued asking the questions that he had prepared. It was clear to him that the three had nothing to do with safety.

He noted that Ivan and Stan were buddies, and that Cheryl was the quiet one who seemed more thoughtful about her answers. She also seemed to be the person in the group that was discounted by the other two.

In just a few minutes less than an hour, Alex thanked Phil for his time and gracious consideration in how he handled the organizational review.

She now had an appreciation of how cautiously Phil was handling his smuggling operation. Johnnie had let her know that Phil's personal record was spotless except for a couple of speeding tickets.

His bodyguards were not as spotless but had not served any time in prison. She expected Lorie and Linda to find that the office help was not aware they worked in a smuggling, gun running organization because the indication was they were running a legitimate goods importing operation.

When she walked out of Phil's office she knocked on the door across the hall and poked her head in and asked if Trey was done with his inspection. She then walked toward the entrance area and signaled Linda and Lorie as she walked out to the van.

Linda saw Alex signal she and Lorie and thanked the person she was talking with for their time. She and Lorie walked out to the van together.

Once they were all in the van, she suggested they go for lunch and review what they had learned.

Trey stopped at the exit of the parking lot and asked where they should go for lunch. He watched as the three persons he had been interviewing walked out to the Range Rover parked by Phil's old SUV. He commented that they were most likely going to be followed.

Alex suggested they drive to the City Hall parking lot and drive in. She had her California sheriff's badge and said that would probably get them into the parking lot. Then once they were in the parking lot they could check to see if their tail left. Once that was, she suggested they go to the waterfront and enjoy a leisurely lunch.

Sitting in the City Hall parking lot, Linda pointed out that the Range Rover parked across from the parking lot entrance was leaving.

Lorie commented that she was ready for lunch.

<u>Chapter 11: Retaliation</u>

Johnnie spent the entire day sorting through that various phone connections. From those connections, he determined that the office workers were just that. They were making daily calls to legitimate goods import companies, handling the daily calls, paying daily bills, or logging in payments to banks. Their calls had no connections with any of the smugglers that called in.

He learned that the bodyguards were just that as well and spent a great deal of time chatting with friends about how great of a job they had as compared with their time in the drug trade.

He was impressed how Phil kept his legitimate business well documented, very legally run with taxes paid and it was disconnected from the smuggling operation. His legal import business focused on finding and importing any goods that was popular with the general public. He was making enough to pay his workers, give them good benefits and still make enough to put a large profit in the bank. He would have been a multi-millionaire from his legitimate business.

He was as well very impressed on how carefully Phil managed his illegitimate business. He was making a huge profit on the goods that he accepted from the Navy, Army, Air Force and National Guard. The fact that his smuggling empire included these armed forces surprised him. He found the volume of stolen military hardware unbelievable. He was not surprised to find a huge sum of money in offshore bank accounts. The accounts were kept separate and designated to indicate with which armed force it was associated. There were several billion dollars in each account. It was a huge sum of money that was earning Phil a phenomenal amount by being invested in the stock market. The money was all untaxed and would be seized by the IRS as soon as they found out about it.

He organized the accounts so that the IRS could seize each of them separately. There was a fifth account that was just in Phil's name that had close to three billion dollars in it. This account was most likely half illegitimate and half legitimate. It as well was kept in investments that spanned the financial investment market. This account would take the IRS more work to determine how much of it was legitimate and had taxes paid on the legitimate money.

During the time Johnnie was digging out all the financial information, Phil was busy trying to figure out who had visited his office. He was sure that more than "inspecting" the safe operation of his business had been underway.

He had his folks look for any bugs, but none were found.

When his bodyguards returned and informed him that the van had entered the main city office building parking lot, he put in a call to the informant that he had there. She called back and let him know that no business safety inspection had been scheduled for his business and in fact that organization was so far behind they only inspected those businesses where a major accident or death had taken place. She added that there was no Alex Evercrest listed as an employee in any of the San Francisco City organizations. This information triggered Phil to ask his secretary to check all San Francisco hotels to see if she was registered in any of them.

Almost by accident Johnnie ran back through all the phone taps that he had set up and was surprised when he discovered that the office support secretary was checking the registration of hotels for Alex. He decided to continue monitoring and was listening when the hotel that Alex and the rest were staying in verified that they had a guest with that name. He immediately put in a call to Alex.

Johnnie's ring let Alex know who was calling. The four of them were sitting in an almost deserted outdoor area of the restaurant in a corner where the rain torrent, which had started when they got there, was not bothering them. She put her phone on speaker mode and set it on the center of the table.

Johnnie began with, "You have all been made." He then explained that he had overheard Phil's support secretary searching hotels for them and was listening when she learned the hotel where they were staying.

Alex thanked him for the heads up and let him know that she and the team would handle the situation.

Johnnie then added that he had found and documented all the offshore bank accounts and had the dollar value for each. He added that there was over ten billion dollars sitting out in those accounts.

Alex thanked him for the good news and asked him to contact Joe Brown and find out who the IRS contact would be that would handle the five offshore accounts and let her know as soon as he possible.

Johnnie ended the conversation by wishing them a safe return to their hotel.

Alex looked around the table and then at the rain that seemed to be giving its all to get to them. She looked at Trey and said that they would need to be super cautious when they returned to the hotel. She added that she would like Linda and Laurie to take the lead when they returned to the hotel and go into the reception area and make sure that there was no one there that they had seen at the business. She would drop them off one block from the hotel and they should walk casually in. She and Trey would drive past the hotel and Trey would walk back and go in next. She would drive into the entrance area and come in last.

The rain seemed to cooperate and stop as they got ready to leave the restaurant. Alex asked that they take off the signs and put them in the carrying case. She laughed and said that they now had their signs for their next unsuccessful try at being elusive sleuths.

Lorie asked what they should do once they were in the lobby.

Alex suggested they go to the area where the internet café was set up and pretend to use one of the computers. If any of the three bodyguards were present they should be ready to protect themselves. She added that she did not think they would be there otherwise the entrance sequence would be the other way around.

As they turned into the street of the hotel entrance, the older SUV parked in front of the dark green Range Rover stood out like a sore thumb to Alex. She asked Trey what he saw.

He replied that some inexperienced group of people interested in finding them were parked along the street leading to the hotel.

Alex said that there was a change in the plan. They would all go in at the same time. She asked that the three get out on the hotel entrance side of the van and she would get out of the driver's side and walk quickly around after they had made it through the front door. She asked Trey to secure the inside area and that once she got in he should keep an eye out for Phil and his bodyguards.

Linda and Lorie should go to the elevators and get one ready to go up.

She was going to go directly to the elevator and they would go to the top floor to her suite.

He should come up after a few minutes. She let him know that the "shave and a haircut knock" was his safe entry signal.

Trey replied that he had her back and he would be up to make sure they had the fire power to face whatever might happen.

When they got to the drop off circle he led the way in and immediately positioned himself so he could see past the van to the sidewalk.

Alex walked past him and walked to the elevator where Linda was holding the door to the elevator open.

Lorie stayed behind and got the next elevator ready to go up.

Trey waited for three minutes and then he turned and walked briskly across the lobby and got into the elevator.

Once they got to Alex's hotel room door, Lorie laughed when Trey gave the "shave and a haircut knock," and was let in.

Alex gave Linda and Lorie each a pillow and said that their role was to throw the pillows at whoever came through the door and then fall to the floor. She went on to say that she and Trey would be the ones doing the shooting if it was necessary.

Phil was sitting in his SUV thinking about what he was going to do. He figured that his smuggling business was at risk, and he needed to do something forceful. He needed to eliminate whoever was trying to either take over his business or trying to close it down. Either way, he was going to have his three bodyguards earn their pay and eliminate all four of them.

He would start with the person who had interviewed him. He would kill her, then go to each of the other rooms and kill each of them. He instructed his three bodyguards to use silencers. He had a universal key card for the hotel that would get them in without the need to knock. He led the way toward the hotel. He noted that the van did not have any signage on it, but he had observed the young black woman get out of the driver's side and was sure she would be in her room. The lack of the signs gave him confidence that he was doing the right thing.

He led the way to the elevators as he waved at the receptionist. He punched the button for the top floor. He wondered what business his first target was in that she could afford to get one of the best rooms in the hotel.

He led the way down the hallway to the room. He handed the key card to Ivan and then stood to the side.

Ivan quietly slid the key card in the lock and then gun in hand he pushed the door open. He was hit in the face by a pillow and reactively fired toward the person that had thrown it. His gun never made it back to the person who was standing in front of him. The last thing he saw was the gun dropping from his hand and the world going black.

Stan, who was standing behind him, raised his gun as Ivan fell to his knees in front of him. He too was surprised by two holes in his chest and the fact that the world was slowly turning dark.

Cheryl did not hesitate she dropped her weapon and ran down the hallway to towards the elevators. She could hear Phil running at her heals. The elevator doors opened immediately. She rushed in with Phil behind her and pressed one. The ride down seemed to take forever and when the doors opened she ran across the lobby and out the door.

Phil caught up with her and suggested they take his SUV and go directly to the private field where he kept his plane. She ran to the Range Rover and retrieved a rifle and her purse. Once in the car she asked the name of the person who had been doing the shooting. When she heard the name she let out a groan and commented that they were both in deep do da because they had just attacked the most successful detective in the country.

Phil asked her about what she was talking.

She replied that Alex Evercrest was a dead shot, had hunted down the worst criminals in the country and was known for always getting the person she chased. She added that they could run but eventually they would be caught. She shook her head and said that it was their death day.

When they got to the airfield, Cheryl said that she was not going with him but was going to stay and walk away into the sun set. She had enough money to tide her over until she could get some low paying job and get a new identity. She wished Phil good luck and began to walk away.

He laughed and said that he had enough money tucked away that he would go to some island in the Pacific and live a life of luxury. He offered Cheryl a ride in comfort to a place of paradise.

Cheryl shook her head, again turned to walk away.

Phil stopped her and said that he had twenty thousand dollars for her as her severance pay. He went to the back of his SUV and gave her a briefcase and wished her good luck.

She thanked him, wished him good luck, turned, walked away, and waved her hand over her head. She left the shot gun in the back of the SUV and walked back toward the highway.

Phil shook his head and got his plane ready for takeoff. He made sure he had enough fuel to get to Hawaii.

Back at the hotel, Alex called in the shooting. She took a picture of the gun in the hallway, marked the spot where it was dropped, carried it back into the apartment and placed it on the sink countertop.

It took the local police about five minutes to show up.

During that time, she put in a call to Jane Stradford, her Illinois Lieutenant Governor boss, and quickly explained the situation.

Jane let her know that she would call the Police Chief in San Francisco and clear the way for her.

Alex then called Harold Zimmerman, the Chicago DEA head and her personal friend and let him know about the situation and the fact that she had uncovered a very successful gun runner.

He let her know that he would alert the San Francisco DEA to get involved in the case and that he would most likely get to her hotel while the police were still there.

When the police arrived, Alex showed her California sheriffs badge and briefly explained the scene. She pointed to her weapon that she had put on the counter next to a gun dropped by one of the attackers who had run away and said that it was the only gun that had been fired.

The policeman in charge asked why no one else had done any shooting.

Trey commented that Alex was exceedingly fast and had never hesitated when the two attackers shot.

Alex shook her head and replied that there was no one else to shoot at for the other three but their weapons were all properly registered.

The coroner arrived and commented on the accuracy of each shot. He asked where she had learned to shoot.

Alex smiled and said that she spent four hours each week at the practice range.

When he heard her name, he shook his head and said that he had watched a recruiting movie at a police convention where the Cincinnati Detective unit featured her. He asked why the two gunmen were after her.

She replied that she was after their boss who had successfully fled the scene with a third potential shooter who had dropped her weapon and run.

She had just finished answering when Audrey Wilson walked in and introduced himself as the San Francisco DEA and asked about the person who she was pursuing.

Immediately after his introduction, the San Francisco Chief of Police, Reily Hinderland, walked in and introduced himself. He commented that he had been asked by her boss to help her out. He looked around and said that it did not seem she needed his protection, but he needed to know more about what led to the shooting.

Alex asked him to sit down, and she would explain to him and Audrey about a large-scale smuggling ring that a Phil Davidson was running.

Chapter 12:Out of the Frying Pan into the Fire

Phil taxied out on the runway for takeoff. He had put in a flight plan to go to Vancouver but planned to revise it once he was in the air when he changed control towers. He figured that would make it harder for anyone trying to figure out where he was going to keep track. He figured that at least in the short term it would give him some breathing room.

Johnnie was tracking Phil's phone and was able to get his position while he was still close to the California coast. He kept a close eye on the direction and when it seemed fixed and just before he lost the phone contact he had the direction figured out.

He knew that Phil was headed toward Hawaii. He was not sure which island but once Phil got close enough to be within range of the Hawaiian phone towers, he would be able to locate him again.

He called Alex and let her know where Phil was headed.

Alex laughed and said that she was looking forward to going there as well. She asked Johnnie to lock down all of Phil's financial accounts so he would be denied access to his money.

Once she was off the phone, she looked over at Linda and Lorie who were sitting on the couch chatting with the police Chief and the DEA rep and asked if Darrel was willing to fly them back to Hawaii.

Linda asked if that was where Phil was headed.

Alex nodded and said she was not sure which island, but they could start out with Maui as the goal and go to a different island if they found out it was some other one.

Lorie laughed and said that Phil was headed toward their favorite location in the world. He should get a break for being so helpful when he was charged with smuggling.

The police Chief said that she would get her weapon back once it was processed and no longer needed.

Alex gave him the office address and asked him to have it shipped there at her expense.

Audry added that he would work with Reily and determine what the DEA would do about the smuggling operation.

Up in the air, Phil put his plane on auto pilot. The time to get to Maui was about five hours so he decided to take a nap and figure out what he would do once he got there. He knew he would continue across the pacific, but he wanted to take a break and get things organized and enjoy the weather on Maui. His house faced west and was on the other side of the road from LOLO cove.

He loved the location and had his house always ready for an impromptu visit. He would go there, decompress and plan what he would do next. He was confident that he had made a clean getaway and had at least a few days on his side.

He figured after a brief stay on the island he would fly on to either Osaka, Japan, or Manila in the Philippines. He had a condo in Osaka and in the Philippines he usually stayed at the Manila Hotel. He figured that if the hotel was good enough for General MacArthur and his family, it was good enough for him.

He was leaning toward Manila because it had more lenient entry requirements as compared to Japan.

Linda and Lorie accompanied Alex and Trey to the airport where they were met by Darrel and led to the plane. Once they were all on board he said that he would fly at max speed, and they should get to Maui close to the time that Phil would get to Hawaii. He added that he would change the destination if they learned which island Phil was headed for. He suggested they all relax, enjoy the refreshments and he would do the hard work of sitting in the cockpit.

Lorie laughed and said that she felt sorry for the huge exertion and strain that he would experience and asked if she should hold his hand to ease his stress.

He said that he would enjoy her holding his hand and he was certain it would reduce the stress he would feel.

Alex said that she was going to take a nap and suggested they all do the same.

Linda called her mother and let her know that she, Lorie, Alex, and Trey were all flying to Maui. She filled her in on the fact that they were in pursuit of a smuggler that was headed towards Hawaii.

Brian came on the line and asked for additional information such as the name of the person and type of airplane he was flying.

Linda gave him Phil's name but said she had no idea what type of plane he was flying. She said that he should check in with Johnnie since he was doing the on-line tracking of Phil.

Brian replied that he would do a little digging to see if he could find out which island Phil was flying into.

Even as Brian was beginning his search for flight information, Johnnie was checking on home ownership on the Islands. He broke down laughing when he found the address of the house registered under Phil's name.

Mary asked him what he was laughing about.

He let her know that Alex was in pursuit of a smuggler who had escaped from San Francisco and was flying to the Hawaiian Islands to escape and on Maui he had a house less than a mile from her waterfront house.

Mary started laughing as well.

He sent a text message with the address to Alex and wished he could be there when she received it to hear her laugh.

He had no sooner sent the message than he got a call from Brian asking what he might have on Phil.

Johnnie shared that address and asked if Brian knew his neighbor.

Brian and Kekoa were sitting together, and both started laughing when they saw the address.

Kekoa made the point that Phil was Alex's next-door neighbor not theirs.

Johnnie shared that he had locked Phil out of access to his bank accounts so money might be a problem for him.

Kekoa said that was great but pointed out that, if Phil was a seasoned smuggler, he most likely had emergency funds stashed away, and he likely had contacts on the Islands that could provide him with additional funding if needed.

A few hours later, as they got close to the island, Alex's phone registered the text message from Johnnie.

She started laughing and read the message out loud.

That had everyone on the plane laughing.

Lorie commented that it was the case of jumping out of the frying pan and into the fire.

When Phil landed he taxied to the private jet parking area where he tied down his plane. He had it serviced, paid to have his gas tank filled and had the engine checked. Once he had the plane ready for takeoff, he took a cab to his beachside home. He relaxed on the drive across the island and stopped at one of his favorite restaurants and had an evening meal. He enjoyed the house special for dinner and had a glass of wine to go along with it.

During his meal he pondered his situation. He was worried about how he was going to handle his business. He figured he should check in with his staff to see if they were still in operation. If so he would contact his network of gun runners and make sure that the equipment and armament they were interested in was made available. The Navy link was dead, but the other connections were still operational.

He would need to make a few changes, but he could run his business from anywhere in the world, so the only inconvenience was having to change his residence.

When the taxi taking him to his home on Makena Road passed the third police car, his radar was on full alert. He asked the taxi driver to take him all the way past Ahihi Cove and then turn around in the parking lot before the continuous lava fields.

He counted three additional police cars just past his house. He decided that somehow they had figured out where he was going. He let the cab driver know that there was a change in plan and to take him back to the airport.

It was definitely time to continue his journey. He would stop at the big island where he had a stash of money, passports and two handguns.

He had seen his top two gunmen go down, so he knew that this detective that was after him was not shy about shooting. The next time they met he planned to be the one to shoot first.

Once he landed on the big island he immediately had his gas tank topped off and the plane serviced.

Once he continued, he would fly at about three quarters speed to ensure that he would have plenty of gas to get to Manila.

He went to the edge of the field in front of his parking space where an old storage shed was standing and opened the lock. He went to the chest that was up against the far wall. He opened it and picked up the satchel that held one hundred and fifty thousand dollars. An old leather briefcase had a set of passports, two revolvers and some ammunition clips. He picked up the two cases and carried them back to the plane.

He took a moment and went over to the vending machines where he purchased several bags of chips, two candy bars and three soft drinks. Not exactly the food that he preferred but he did not want to take the time to go and buy something else. He returned to his plane and put in a flight plan to Oahu.

He had decided to fly to Manila but would put in a second flight plan later or not put in a flight plan change at all.

As Phil took off from the big island, Darrel brought the plane in for a smooth landing on Maui and taxied over to the hanger. He helped everyone off and pointed to a black van that was parked near the entrance.

Annie and Brian were walking toward them. They all shared hugs and then Brian said that he had the police out trying to apprehend Phil but so far they had not been able to do so.

Alex thanked him and let him know that Johnnie had tracked Phil to Maui and then had tracked him to the big island where he stayed for a little over an hour. He was now heading across the Pacific towards the Philippines.

She added that what she would like to do was to get a search warrant to search his Maui house to see if she could find something that would give her a clue where in the Philippines he was going.

Brian made a call and afterwards said that they could drive to Phil's house and a search warrant would be there when they arrived.

During the search of the house, Linda kept commenting on what a great place it was and how she would love to have a place like it.

Lorie held up a brochure featuring the Manila Hotel and said she thought she had Phil's destination.

Alex said they were through with the search of the house and should plan on getting on the plane and heading for Manila.

Trey said he was game, but he reminded everyone that they had a dinner invitation that evening.

Linda said that she would let Darryl know that they wanted to take off bright and early the next morning.

Lorie nodded and said that she was not going to miss a free dinner at her favorite restaurant and planned to chow down.

While the dinner on Maui was being enjoyed, Phil landed in Manila and after having his plane serviced and tied down, he headed to one of his favorite local restaurants for a decent meal. He planned to enjoy it and then go and check in to the Manila Hotel, take a shower and enjoy a good night's sleep. He had concluded that running to escape was exhausting.

He shook his head and remembered Cheryl's comment about Alex Evercrest always getting the person she chased. He was beginning to understand the comment and hoped that he had been able to shake the pursuit.

The next morning, after breakfast, he tried to access his primary offshore account. He was surprised that he was not able to do so. He sequentially tried the other five accounts only to learn that he was locked out of them as well. He wondered who had the power to do such a thing. He figured he would be able to get them reinstated if he went to each bank in person. He figured he would do so after he had made sure he had made his escape. In the short term he had one hundred and fifty thousand dollars to tide him over.

He spent the afternoon contacting his customers and arranging deliveries of weapons and other materials in which they were interested. He went to a bank that was walking distance from the hotel and opened an account and asked his customers to send the money there. He put five thousand dollars into the account and also rented a security box where he put one hundred forty thousand and his extra pistol.

The next thing he wanted to do was to find a place outside of the downtown Manila area where he could set up a more permanent residence

The next morning when Alex and the rest of the team arrived at the Maui airport, Darryl asked how fast they wanted to get to Manila.

He let them know that if they wanted the top speed, he would need to put his long-distance extra fuel tank in the luggage compartment. If he flew at his normal cruise speed, he would not need the extra fuel.

Alex said that his normal cruise speed would be fine. She added that she was more interested in getting to Manila safely.

Once they were all on board, Alex got on the phone and talked with Johnnie. She asked him to verify the arrival of Phil to the Manila Hotel and see if he could find out the room number.

Johnnie said he would get her the information. He felt good about his involvement in the chase. He also felt good about his ability to identify the rest of the smuggling network participants. He was sure that his follow the money trail was going to pay off as well.

What he felt best about was that in the past week he had gone out on the Golden Goose fishing twice, had caught several bass and had slept in his own bed every night. His move to Evanston was proving to be a great choice.

Alex's second call was to Joe Brown to verify the IRS agents that would be involved. She let Joe know that she was interested in Phil's Maui home and his airplane as part of the finder's reward. She figured it was better to ask early.

Joe said that he was sure both the IRS and the various military financial people that would be involved would be pleased to reward her with physical property since that was always harder to handle than just handling the money.

The final call was to Matt to let him know where she was going and to see when it would be a good time to call so she could talk to Aurea.

Matt laughed and said any time other than three in the morning would be great.

<u>Chapter 13: End of the Line</u>

Phil woke up, left the hotel, went to the airport, and flew north to Laoag to look at several places along the Padsan River. He had previously looked at places there and knew a realtor there that he contacted. He found the place he wanted and put down enough money to hold it, but he realized he would need to get his accounts unfrozen if he wanted to close the deal. He would try once again to access his other accounts, but he realized he could easily redirect the flow of any new payments to his new bank account, and he would have the money he needed in just a few weeks. This realization put him at ease, and he felt that he was going to be successful in his getaway.

He flew back to Manila where he once again had his plane fueled and prepped. He then took a taxi to a restaurant near the Manila Hotel. He went in, ordered, and enjoyed a nice traditional lunch of Seafood Adobo. He felt he was successful in his escape, in finding a new home and in re-aligning his business.

His lunch was one of the best he had recently eaten. He took the time to call his customers, went for a leisurely walk in the park on his way back to his Manila Hotel room.

Everything was going as planned and he felt good.

Suddenly he stopped dead in his tracks. He realized that the tall white guy with a green ball cap ahead of him was the same guy that had been part of the fake security inspection of his office back in San Francisco.

He spotted the black female who had interviewed him walking about ten feet ahead of the green ball cap guy.

He figured the two young females following a little farther behind were part of the group.

He paused for a moment and made sure his weapon was fully loaded. He now wished he had the second pistol he had put in the safety deposit box. He grabbed a full clip with his left hand and stepped into the bushes. He took aim at the center of the black female's back and fired three times. He then immediately shot the tall guy three times in the back.

He put his second clip in his gun and the next four shots were for the two women. One of them had turned and got shot twice in the chest the other got shot in the back.

He then turned and ran away keeping the bushes between him and the four he had just shot. He almost knocked over a young mother pushing her baby carriage. He knew he needed to get back to his plane and once again figure out how to get away. He kept repeating, "How, How, How as he ran toward a cab."

Alex staggered forward when the bullets hit her in the back. She turned to shoot but did not see her target. She hesitated to shoot at all because the park was full of young women and children. She saw that Trey had been hit as well and like her, he had turned to return fire but did not. She looked over to where Linda and Lorie were checking on each other.

Linda had turned when the shooting started and got hit twice in the chest. She staggered back and bumped into Lorie.

Lorie had been hit twice in the back and was trying to recover when Linda bumped into her. She hugged Linda and asked if she was alright.

Linda said that she would live but she did not feel alright at the moment, and she now understood how Lorie had felt the first time she had been shot.

Alex had not expected to be ambushed in the middle of the busy park. She hesitated only a moment and then put in a call to Darrel at the airport and asked him to keep Phil from being able to take off in his plane and that she and the rest of the team were on the way over.

She was surprised that the shooting seemed to have gone unnoticed or at least ignored by the people in the park. She checked with Trey, Linda, and Lorie to see if anyone was going to have more than bruises.

Lorie replied that she was really upset at getting shot without a chance of shooting back. She complained that the last time she was shot, her ribs hurt for a week. Now she was going to have a pain in her back for the next two weeks and her suit jacket and blouse had multiple holes through them. She said that she was ready to shoot Phil the next time they met.

Linda added that she now knew what it felt like to be shot, and it was worse than the proverbial kick of a mule. She had turned when the shooting started and had been hit twice in the chest.

Trey said that he had gone through getting shot enough times that he was focused on getting even and wanted to get to Phil's plane.

Alex hailed a taxi and asked the driver to get to the airport as fast as possible.

Darrel had let Alex know that he would make sure that Phil would not be able to take off. He walked over to where Phil's jet was tied down and checked that the tie downs were designed to be locked. He walked back to his plane and opened his toolbox, took out two locks, walked back to Phil's jet and put the locks on the cables attached to the wings.

He then walked back to his jet, locked everything up and went into the hangar's snack room and bought a bag of chips and a soft drink. He had been about to go to lunch but now figured he would wait for Alex and the rest of them to get to the hangar. He called Alex back and let her know that Phil would not be taking off in his plane.

Phil walked briskly to the edge of the park to a cab that was parked in the shade of a large banyan tree. He got in, asked the driver to drive to the hotel and wait a moment while he went to get his suitcase.

He had expected the police to show up, but the park seemed quiet.

He figured the four he had shot were either dead or critically wounded but he made sure that the four were nowhere in sight and then walked briskly to the elevator and took it up to his floor. He entered his room and hurriedly packed his bag. He looked around to make sure he was not leaving anything that would give away where he was going. He pulled his bag to the elevator, went down, and returned to the waiting cab. His current plan was to fly to Laoag and stay in the condo that he had agreed to lease. He hoped that the third time would be the time to make his getaway.

He asked the driver to take him to the airport where the private planes parked. He tried to relax during the thirty-minute drive but kept looking behind the taxi to make sure no one was following.

While Phil was getting prepared to leave, Alex ran over to a taxi and asked the taxi driver to get them to the private plane area of the airport as quickly as possible. When they arrived, she thanked the taxi driver for a very exciting ride and gave him a big tip.

She saw that Phil's plane was still there and Phil was not in sight. They all walked into the hanger area and over to the snack room.

Darrel stood up and said that he was glad to see them and added that he thought they had arrived before Phil because he had expected Phil to come in and go to the office to ask why his plane was locked down.

Alex thanked Darrel, turned asked Linda and Lorie if they were feeling up to confronting Phil.

Lorie asked if it was OK for her to shoot him.

Alex laughed, shook her head, and said that they would first try to arrest him and only resort to any shooting if he pulled a weapon.

Phil looked out of the taxi as it arrived at the private plane hangar. He paid the driver and gave him a tip for having waited and wished him a good day. He then pulled his bag over to where his plane was parked. He took his bag into the plane and decided that he would fire it up and get the air conditioning going to cool down the interior. He then went out to release the tie downs. When he got to the wing tie downs he realized that they were locked on. He wondered why that had been done.

He looked around suspiciously but saw no one. He reentered the plane, got his gun, made sure he had reloaded it and put the extra clips into his pocket. He then headed for the hangar to see who had the keys to the locks. He walked into the main office and asked about the tie down locks.

The young female clerk asked him to wait for a moment. She turned and asked, two young men in blue coveralls who were sitting and chatting, if they had locked down the plane in question.

Both of them shook their heads in the negative and said that they had not locked down any planes.

In his frustration, Phil pulled his gun and said that he did not care who had locked down the plane, but they should get a bolt cutter and cut the locks off because he was ready to leave.

The two stood up, held up their hands and said he should follow them out to where the tools were, and they would go out and cut off the locks.

Phil put his gun back into his pocket and followed the two out of the back door of the office.

Alex saw Phil exiting from the office. She quietly said they should leave the snack room and spread out. They would follow the three out to the plane and see if they could surprise Phil and get the upper hand. She reminded everyone that she would do the talking and if necessary the initial shooting.

Phil followed the two hanger personnel out to his plane. They walked over to the far wing cable and cut the lock off.

He was following them around to the wing near the planes entrance door when he realized that the four people he had shot and thought he had killed were spread out in front of him.

The was thoroughly surprised and shook up. He told the two mechanics to stop. He stood behind them and called out that he was getting on the plane and leaving. He said that he would shoot the mechanics if anyone tried to stop him. He guided the two mechanics over to the wing and told the one holding the bolt cutter to cut the lock.

After the cable fell to the ground, Phil looked to where the four were standing and realized that each of them was pointing their weapon toward him. He was fully shielded by the two mechanics and felt safe. He decided to shoot the four and then get on the plane.

He raised his weapon to shoot the black female first when magically he watched his gun fall out of his hand. He realized that he had not heard the sound of the bullet being fired as his world winked out.

Alex had been closely watching Phil, when she saw him glance her way and begin to point his gun at her, she fired one shot. She watched the gun fall from Phil's hand as a small hole just above his nose began to bleed. Phil's knees seemed to buckle as he fell forwards between the two mechanics. He landed in a prone position as if he was bowing to her. It reminded her of the first person she had ever killed who ended up in the same position.

The two mechanics bolted away as Phil fell limply to the ground. Once they got past the four, they both stopped to look back.

Trey walked over to where Phil was now lying face down, then looked at Alex and said that once again she had not given him a chance to shoot.

Lorie commented that it was not fair because she had asked first to be the one to shoot Phil.

Alex asked the two mechanics to call the police.

She looked at Lorie and told her that she had no choice because Phil was targeting her first.

She called Captain Kirpatrick back in San Diego, explained what had happened and asked him if he knew anyone in the Navy stationed in Manila that might be able to give her a hand.

The Captain said that he knew several of the brass there and he would give them a call. He asked where they could get in touch with her.

She said that she would most likely be sitting in a police station trying to explain the situation to the local police, but they could get in touch with her on her phone.

She turned and suggested that Darrel take everyone for a flight along the coast and return after a couple of hours. She would stay and handle the local police.

Linda spoke up and said that she was not going anywhere. They had all been shot at, they had all been ready to shoot again and she was not worried about the local police.

Trey smiled and said that she knew better than to suggest he leave.

Lorie laughed and said that the only thing she was mad about was that she was not the one who had shot Phil and that she wanted to finish this up, enjoy a traditional Philippine dinner and go out shopping for new clothes to replace the suit she was wearing that had two holes in the back.

The police seemed to arrive in mass. They asked what had happened and who shot the person on the ground.

Alex became the spokesperson for the group as she handed her gun to the officer. She explained that Phil had been fleeing from the US as he tried to avoid being arrested for smuggling. She described his flight to Hawaii and then his escape from there to the Philippines. She shared the fact that she and her team followed him and that he had ambushed them at the park near the Manila Hotel.

She then explained he was in the process of trying once again to escaped via his plane. She pointed to the two mechanics, said that their lives had been threatened and when Phil raised his gun to shoot her, she had shot and killed him before he could shoot.

One of the mechanics said something in Tagalog and the police looked over at Alex and asked her how she had been able to shoot and miss the two mechanics.

Alex smiled and said there was an inch between their heads, so she had plenty of room.

The policeman said that he now understood why the two mechanics kept talking about the fact that they thought they were going to die but that a miracle had happened. He added that the miracle was that she was an excellent shot.

Alex nodded and said that she would not have taken the shot if she thought she would miss.

The policeman took a call, looked at Alex and said that he had been instructed to take her to the main police station for a debriefing.

The ride to the station took about thirty minutes. They arrived and were met at the curb by two Navy officers. One was a captain and the second was a lieutenant. The captain said that he had been asked to help her in any manner that she needed.

Alex thanked him and said that she just needed to make sure that the local police knew she was on a legitimate chase of a dangerous criminal that had been running a smuggling ring. She had registered her teams weapons as required by the Philippine government and had entered with all the proper paperwork. She just wanted to make sure the local police did not overreact because she had killed the person she had been chasing.

The Captain let her know that he had been informed by his friend in San Diego of the situation. He had contacted the head of the police department and had set up a meeting with him.

Alex thanked him. She looked at Trey, Linda, and Lorie and asked them if they were ready for the meeting.

Trey said that he would like a moment to call home then he was set.

Linda and Lorie made a similar request.

Alex smiled and said she had a couple of calls to make as well.

They all walked over into the shade of a large tree and stood making their calls.

Her first call was to Johnnie let him know what had happened and then asked him to get everything wrapped up and ready for the IRS. She let him know that she wanted the jet plane and the house.

Johnnie said that he had already been in contact with the IRS, and they had indicated that they were quite happy to grant her all the physical assets that Phil owned that was associated with the smuggling ring. They had also let him know that they would only be getting a fifteen percent finders reward because the military branches wanted the money to make up for their smuggling losses.

Alex laughed and said that fifteen percent of twelve billion was how much?

She asked if he was going to be satisfied with his share of two hundred and twenty-five million before taxes share or was he going to fight for a higher percentage.

Johnnie laughed and said that he had gone from sleeping under Cincinnati over passes to now worrying about how much tax he was paying for a fortune. He said that he would be very happy with just another tray of her cookies.

Alex agreed to bake the cookies once she was back in Evanston.

After hanging up she called Matt, who asked what was wrong. She responded that everything was fine.

He asked if she realized that once again it was three in the morning.

Alex apologized and quickly explained what had happened and that she was just calling to let him know she was OK and that she loved him.

Matt thanked her for calling. He said that in the morning he would let Aurea, and the rest of the family know what had happened.

Alex hung up, looked around to find everyone ready to go in and talk with the police.

Ron Mueller

160

<u>Chapter 14: First Case Aftereffects</u>

The discussion at the police station lasted about two hours. Alex was pleased with the help she got from the Navy Officers and invited them out to dinner. They both thanked her but declined because they both had their family to get home to.

Alex suggested they all go out shopping first and have dinner at the usual late starting time that was the habit in the Philippines.

Linda suggested they all go back to the hotel, take a shower, and change clothes.

Lorie said that sounded like a great idea.

Trey said that a couple of hours in a hot shower would feel good on his back.

Alex nodded and said that they certainly deserved a few moments to recover. Then they could do their shopping and if they still felt up to it they could do dinner.

The shopping turned out to be a great way to decompress from the tension of the day. Each of them were able to find several new outfits. Trey said he was happy to find the variety of hats that fit him. He said that he had bought hats for Matt, her father, mother, Johnnie and a special one for Aurea. He had also replaced his jacket, and shirt that had four holes in them.

Alex was also able to buy several outfits for Aurea.

At dinner she got a call from Johnnie letting her know that he had expedited the transfer of ownership of the plane and the house on Maui. He had also accepted Phil's office building in San Francisco and a sixty-foot yacht that was anchored in Maui. He said that he hoped that his decision to accept the physical items as part of the reward was acceptable.

Alex let him know that she thought he was doing a great job interfacing with the IRS and would make sure to reward him with several trays of cookies. She heard Mary comment that Johnnie didn't need fattening up. Alex asked Johnnie to find a pilot qualified to fly the companies new jet plane and to rent a spot at the Executive airport where they could keep it.

She hung up and let Linda and Lorie know about the house and yacht in Maui.

Linda came over and gave her a hug and said that she was looking forward to being her Maui neighbor.

Lorie commented that they would probably take the yacht to Oahu where they could use it when they were there on weekends. She said that she figured it was likely a two and a half hour trip between Kihei and Honolulu ant they could also use it to go home on weekends.

Alex then called Matt and was able to speak to him, Aurea, and her mother. She let them know that she was returning late the following day.

She then made plans with Trey, Linda, and Lorie to all go back to Evanston so they could have an official business meeting. She wanted to review all the packages going to the IRS and to see what loose ends needed to be closed as part of the case.

She arranged with the Navy captain to get Phil's body returned to California.

Darrel let them know that the shortest flight back was through Portland where he would need to refuel before they flew on to Evanston Executive airport.

Alex commented that she planned to catch up on her sleep.

The flight back was long but uneventful. They landed and agreed that the next day they would all meet at the office at ten.

Trey said that Lindsey was at Alex's mother's house, so he was going with her to her house.

Alex and Trey took a taxi to her house. She had a surge of fond memories as the taxi drove through the tunnel made by the tree branches over the driveway. When Aurea came running out to greet her she felt a surge of love and jumped out to give her a hug. She took a moment to pay the taxi driver and then picked Aurea up and carried her toward the front door.

Matt came out and gave her a hug, Aurea got down, took her hand, and said that everyone was out by the pool.

She got hugs from everyone and the was led to the table that had a variety of food. She looked down the table at three meat offerings. There was prime rib roast, coconut shrimp and a simple pan-fried salmon as the choice of meats. She also saw that there was a dish of sliced tomatoes with vinegar, olive oil and parsley which was one of her favorites. She decided on a thin slice of prime rib and a few slices of tomato.

After she had her plate she took it over to where everyone was sitting and asked Johnnie how his work with the IRS was going. He smiled and said that he had been able to get them to up their reward percentage to twenty percent and he had been able to get the deeds to the physical parts of the reward.

Alex said that she would bake a couple of trays of cookies so the team would have them for their ten o'clock in the morning meeting.

Matt let her know that the Golden Goose was now being rented out three days a week and would be turning a profit if business kept up at the current rate. He was reserving Saturdays for going out fishing with Aurea, but they preferred going out on the Minnow, so the Golden Goose was going out on Saturdays with Dexter as the captain. So far he had kept Sundays open for family use.

Alex asked how the construction of the restaurant was going.

Her mother spoke up and said that the kitchen was done and scheduled for a trial. She added that she was going to cook their Sunday dinner after the Golden Goose came in from fishing. The fish would be cleaned in the kitchen cleaning station and prepared for roasting, deep frying, and grilling. She commented that this would let her test the ovens, the grill, and the deep fryer. She would also serve a lamp chop for each person.

Alex said that she would make Sunday's fishing a celebration of a very successful start to the new businesses. She figured that between the two businesses she would have twelve people going out on the Golden Goose.

Rose-Anne said that was a great idea and she would make sure there was enough of everything.

Johnnie let her know that he had found a pilot for her jet that lived locally that she might want to invite to verify that he was the person she would want as a permanent hire.

Alex asked Aurea to bring her the small blue suitcase that had a bow on the handle.

Aurea rushed out and came back with the bag.

Alex unzipped it and took out two dresses, some black slacks and three blouses, and a black suit outfit.

Aurea looked at each and excitedly said she was going to try them on and see how they fit.

During the time she was doing that, Trey went and got the caps that he had brought as gifts and gave them to Russel, Johnnie, Matt, Rose-Anne and one for Aurea that said, "I only fish for the big ones."

Aurea smiled and said that was exactly the hat she needed.

Rose-Anne gave him a hug and was about to make a comment about not getting a gift from her daughter when Alex pulled out an apron that announced it was being worn by the greatest chef in the world.

The following morning, Alex was down early for breakfast. Not long after Aurea and Matt came down the stairs into the kitchen.

Rose-Anne was taking breakfast orders and delivering them one at a time.

Aurea said she was looking forward to fishing the next day on the Minnow and asked if Alex was going to fish.

Alex said that she wouldn't miss it. She planned to catch enough fish to make sure there would be plenty for the following day. She smiled and added that all the fish they caught would be cleaned by the new kitchen help that her mother had hired so it would be the right time for each of them to catch their limit.

Matt laughed and said he hoped fishing would be great for all of them.

Rose-Anne said that she too hoped that fishing would be good. She added that she would hate to have to serve pizza if they didn't catch enough fish.

Russel had been listening to the banter and said that he would prepare all the poles that afternoon and make sure they got put on the Minnow. He added that he would put in an order for the bait with Dexter to make sure they had a good variety to choose from.

Matt took Aurea's hand and said that it was time to get to the end of the driveway and catch the bus.

Alex jumped up and said the she was coming too.

Aurea took her hand, and they walked down the lane holding hands. She knew she was one of the luckiest girls in her school. She had parents, grandparents, and close friends all of whom loved her. She thought school was easy and fishing on weekends was grand.

After Aurea got on the bus, as Alex and Matt walked back toward the house, Matt brought up the fact that the money that Johnnie had mentioned was well beyond anything he had ever dreamt would happen to them. He wondered if she needed to continue her investigative business.

Alex thought for a moment and said that the business certainly would be able to choose only the cases that interested one of the principles, and she could see setting up a charity that they could all get involved in that would fill in the quiet times on the investigation side. She added that she wanted to do more with her charity, "Helping Hands." Part of the settlement was the smuggling operation, and she planned to turn that into a charity that would seek to help the homeless in the San Francisco area. She looked at Matt, squeezed his hand and said that she was going to make sure that she focused on him and Aurea more and the business a little less.

Matt gave her a hug and said that it made him feel like he was being listened to.

The next day's fish count on the Minnow hit a record high. The bass seemed to enjoy every type of bait, and everyone caught their limit.

Rose-Anne laughed when Aurea said that they had all celebrated the fact that they did not have to clean their own fish.

Alex added that since her mother would be busy supervising the cleaning of the fish, her father had invited them to the pizza shop for lunch and to his favorite Italian restaurant for dinner.

Rose-Anne said that she would be going to dinner with them and afterwards they should enjoy desert by the pool.

The Sunday fishing trip on the Golden Goose was attended by all the company personnel and their significant others. Nolan had flown in and made the Saturday night desert session and joined in on the Sunday fishing outing. Everyone kept lunch on the light side in anticipation of the evening dinner.

Alex decided that the light lunch had been appropriate because her mother prepared the lake trout and bass in three different fashions. It seemed to her that her mother was becoming a better chef by the day. She listened to everyone say how delicious everything was. By dinner's end the fish had been devoured and everyone was ready for the rhubarb-strawberry pie and the to die for mud pie. She watched Aurea splash around in the pool and felt that she had made the right decision in moving home, buying the marina, and setting up her own investigation agency.

Marisa let her know that the new pilot was not able to make the fishing trip on the Golden Goose but would be in on Monday.

The focus of the evening's discussion was the amazing amount of money the first case for *Evercrest, McGregor, Smith and O'Brien* had pulled in.

She gave Linda and Lorie, the two junior partners, the credit for getting the case in the door. She added that as soon as the two drew their paintings about the case they were in line for a promotion.

On Monday Alex called the team together to review their case and how they were closing it.

She again thanked Linda and Lorie for bringing the Navy smuggling case in the door.

She thanked Johnnie for finding out who the king pin of the smuggling operation was and his ability to find the offshore bank accounts and how much was in each one.

She commented that they had tracked down Phil and in the end he had tried to kill all of them. She made the point that only one person had not been tracked down and she was not looking to track that person down because Johnnie had found her and learned she was going to a local college to become a nurse. It appeared that she had decided to seek a more meaningful life. Alex added that they would keep an eye on her to see that she stuck with her new life.

Cheryl, the person Alex was talking about, had abandoned being a bodyguard and was currently working in a used bookstore just north of San Francisco. She had enrolled in a local junior college and was working towards a nursing degree and hoped to get accepted at one of the many California state colleges. She wondered what had happened to Phil. He had given her twenty thousand dollars when she had declined to fly with him to Hawaii.

She figured he would be the one that would get chased and she believed he would get caught. She hoped that she was low enough on the totem pole to be ignored. She would have been happy if she could have heard how she was discussed in the meeting that determined her fate. As it was she was happy to be pursuing something that made her life meaningful to her.

Alex pointed out that everyone in the organization would get an equal share of the IRS finders reward.

Marisa asked if everyone included her.

Alex smiled, nodded, and said everyone meant everyone and in this case she was including Darrel who had flown them and had helped in the capture of Phil. She added that it made all of them very rich and she planned to make sure that the cases that they took on in the future would be of the most challenging kind that were found few and far between.

This meant that they would be very bored unless they took on some personal endeavors such as her spending more time focused on her Helping Hands organization, converting Stan's smuggling business into a charity, and spending more time with Matt and Aurea.

Trey spoke up and said that he would love to help with the Helping Hands program because he had a lot of history with the property that the physical part of that organization was located.

Linda smiled and said that she was going to spend a great deal of time getting painting lessons from her mother.

Lorie said that she was going to expand the art gallery in Cincinnati and spend a great deal of time using the companies new yacht trying to make it into a going business like the Golden Goose. That would allow her to pursue another career and also spend time with Nolan.

Johnnie added that he planned to take it easy, go out on the Golden Goose as often as possible and eat oatmeal and chocolate chip cookies baked by his most favorite detective.

Marisa said she was amazed and still in shock that she was getting an equal share like everyone else. She said that she had a couple of trips she wanted to take but what she looked forward to the most was working with all of them and becoming a true team member.

Alex looked around the table and complemented all of them for working so well together and she was sure they would continue to have each other's backs.

The bell from the lobby rang.

Marisa excused herself and went out to see who it might be. She found a rather handsome, young looking young man who introduced himself as Riley Lansberry. He said that he was coming in to be interviewed for the position of pilot of the company plane. Marisa introduced herself, smiled and said that he was just in time, and she would take him to the conference room where the interview would take place.

Linda watched as Marisa led a handsome man into the meeting and introduced him as Riley Lansberry who had come to be interviewed for the position of company pilot.

Alex asked if everyone wanted to be part of the interview. Trey, Johnnie, and Lorie all said they were ready for a break and got up and followed Marisa out of the conference room.

Linda looked at Riley, felt an immediate attraction and said she was staying.

Alex welcomed Riley and asked him how long he had been flying. He shared the fact that he had just graduated from flight school. He had flown helicopters in the Navy and had a brief tour in Iraq where he was the pilot for an observation helicopter. He had been lucky not to see any direct fighting. On his return he had immediately entered flight school to be a pilot of commercial jets.

Linda asked him why he should be hired with so little experience.

He shook his head and said that it didn't sound like he was making the right impression. He wanted to make sure that the two of them looked at him as a mature person who would do a great job. His focus was always on safety and making sure that what he was flying was in top condition. He could overhaul most jet engines on the small commercial planes, and he was a pilot not a flight mechanic. His hours flying jet planes was on the low side, but his skill was at the top in his class.

Alex asked him how he knew Darrel Quinly.

Riley smiled and said that he was a friend of his older brother. His brother and Darrel had attended the University of Illinois. Darrel had been one of the reasons he had enlisted, received a degree at Illinois and had become a helicopter pilot. He had recently gone on to become qualified to fly small commercial jets.

Alex smiled and said that he was indeed making the right impression and that she was hiring him, and his first assignment was to travel to Manila and fly the company's new jet airplane back. He would fly there first class, spend as much time there getting use to the plane as he saw necessary and then fly it back.

Linda smiled and said that she was going to escort him there and then fly back with him. She asked when he was planning to leave for Manila. She had felt an immediate draw to him, and she planned on following through to find out if it was real.

Alex noted the attraction and hoped that Linda had found the person that would make her whole.

The End

About the Author

Ronald E. Mueller
remwriter95@gmail.com

Ron grew up in what is now Flint River State Park in Southeast Iowa. The 170-year-old house Ron lived in is built into a hillside. It faces a 125-foot-high cliff towering over the little Flint River. The house and the land talked to him about; the passing of time, the struggle to conquer the land, the struggles people faced and the wonder of nature.

He climbed the cliffs, crawled into the caves, dove from the swimming rock, collected clams from the bottom of the pond, gigged and skinned frogs for their legs. He trapped muskrats for fur, hunted raccoon in the dead of night, and with only a stick hunted rabbits in the dead of winter.

His young life was outdoors, and nature tested him.

He walked to a one room stone schoolhouse uphill both ways. A stern but warm-hearted teacher, Mrs. Henry was instrumental in shaping his character as she shepherded him from the fourth to the eighth grade. A Montessori before its time. It was a great way to grow up.

His experiences inter-twined with snippets of fantasy lend themselves to the adventures he leads the reader through.

Ron Mueller

<u>Characters in the Story</u>

Brian	Rory	O'Neill	Main character
Marian	Lilian	Nelson	Psychologist/Psychiatrists/Anakē
Alec		Daily	Prostitute Mother
Kaia		Keahi	runs the daycare Pukalani
Anakoni		Keahi	Husband
Pukalani		Keahi	Window of heaven - home Brian grows
Sister Ella			nun in the small church
Linda		Scots	Mother-Loveland Park
Stanley	Manfred	Scots	Father
Annie	Lorie	Scots	Missing girl
Linda		Scots	Annies older daughter
Lorie		Scots	Annies second daughter
Alex	Cathy	Evercrest	Cincinnati Police Detective
Matthew	Timothy	Knolton	Alex's suitor
David		Kalama	"the torch" Hawaiian Detective
Malia		Aukai	"Seafarer" Hawaiian Detective
Leilani		Dickens	Hawaiian Detective
Kekoa		Ikaika	Hawiian It
Anela		Kamaka	Kekoa's soul mate
Bailey			Anela's friend
Johnnie		Smith	Key Character
Mary		Higgins	Johnnie's new Philadelphia "friend"
John	S.	Williams	Lawyer that was abused
Hanna		Waverly	John's mate
Joe		Brown	Ohio IRS Unit leader
Jorge		Cruz	New replacement DEA
Harold		Zimmerman	DEA Chicago
Angelica		Calderon	Angel on the Hill
Marvin		Hestor	Van Driver for Brian
Kala			Hawaiian for Princess
Jane	Elousie	Stradford	Lieutenant Governor
Trey		McGregor	Alex's Detective Partner

Lindsey	McGregor	Wife
Nolan	McGregor	Son
Rose-Anne	Germain Evercrest	Alex's mother
Russel	Johnson Evercrest	Alex's father
Marisa	Eberly	Suport in new business
Lydia		Navy Lieutenant
Bilan	Kirpatrick	Captain at the San Diego Naval Baes
Lt.	Halloway	Navy Lieutenant
Darrel	Quinly	Pilot of the privat jet Brian leased.
Kaleo	Palakiko	District Attorney
Captain Saure		Coast Guard
Phil	Davidson	Arms Distributor
Ivan	Lubosky	bodyguard # 1
Stan	Newbury	bodyguard # 2
Cheryl	Hinderman	bodyguard # 3
Riley	Lansberry	Pilot for the new company plane
Jason	Shephard	Alex's first boss

Published by: Around the World Publishing LLC.

QR Links to
ATWP.US web site